SPECIAL MESSAGE TO READERS

THE ULVERSCROFT FOUNDATION
(registered UK charity number 264873)
was established in 1972 to provide funds for research, diagnosis and treatment of eye diseases. Examples of major projects funded by the Ulverscroft Foundation are:-

- The Children's Eye Unit at Moorfields Eye Hospital, London
- The Ulverscroft Children's Eye Unit at Great Ormond Street Hospital for Sick Children
- Funding research into eye diseases and treatment at the Department of Ophthalmology, University of Leicester
- The Ulverscroft Vision Research Group, Institute of Child Health
- Twin operating theatres at the Western Ophthalmic Hospital, London
- The Chair of Ophthalmology at the Royal Australian College of Ophthalmologists

You can help further the work of the Foundation by making a donation or leaving a legacy. Every contribution is gratefully received. If you would like to help support the Foundation or require further information, please contact:

THE ULVERSCROFT FOUNDATION
The Green, Bradgate Road, Anstey
Leicester LE7 7FU, England
Tel: (0116) 236 4325

website: www.foundation.ulverscroft.com

A GERMAN SUMMER

When her younger sister Stella disappears, it's up to Jo to find her and bring her home. It soon becomes clear that Stella has gone to Germany to stay with Jo's childhood pen-pal Max, with whom she has secretly been corresponding. As the sisters enjoy Max's hospitality in his splendid castle, Jo discovers that the grown-up man is very different to the boy she once knew — and very attractive, too. But staying in Germany is not an option, especially when her ill mother needs her back home . . .

Books by Carol MacLean
in the Linford Romance Library:

WILD FOR LOVE
RESCUE MY HEART
RETURN TO BARRADALE
THE JUBILEE LETTER
FROZEN HEART
JUNGLE FEVER
TO LOVE AGAIN
A TEMPORARY AFFAIR
FINDING HER PERFECT FAMILY
HER HIGHLAND LAIRD
SHADOWS AT BOWERLY HALL
HEART OF THE MOUNTAIN

CAROL MACLEAN

A GERMAN SUMMER

Complete and Unabridged

LINFORD
Leicester

First published in Great Britain in 2017

First Linford Edition
published 2017

A catalogue record for this book is available from the British Library.

ISBN 978–1–4448–3329–4

Published by
F. A. Thorpe (Publishing)
Anstey, Leicestershire

Set by Words & Graphics Ltd.
Anstey, Leicestershire
Printed and bound in Great Britain by
T. J. International Ltd., Padstow, Cornwall

This book is printed on acid-free paper

1

'Gone? What do you mean gone?' Andy looked shocked — but was that also a flash of guilt passing over his mobile face?

Jo sighed. 'Tell me you didn't, Andy.'

'Didn't what?'

'Forget the innocent act. You did, I can tell. You asked Stella to marry you, didn't you?'

Now the guilt spread visibly across his face. He rubbed his nose and echoed Jo's sigh. 'I love her. I want to spend the rest of my life with her.'

Jo pushed past him into his house and sat on the sofa, waiting for him to join her. He shuffled in like a naughty schoolboy.

'I didn't think she'd do a runner. Do you think that's it, then — that I've lost her?'

He looked on the verge of tears. Jo

took pity on him. 'It's not the first time she's disappeared. She'll be back. She loves you, but she's scared of commitment. Stella believes herself to be a free spirit.'

What Jo believed was that her little sister needed a good talking-to. Stella had finally, in Jo's opinion, found a wonderful boyfriend. Andy was kind and gentle, worked hard, and had a nice house and well-paid job. But her sister seemed determined to mess things up for herself. Whenever things got tough, Stella took off. She'd put their mother Maureen and Jo, older by ten years, through a lot of anguish over the years of bringing her up.

'So, what now?' Andy asked, looking at Jo as if she were in charge.

That was Jo's problem: she was the sensible one in a family of three women. Her mother coped well on a daily basis but was fragile when it came to her love for her girls. The loss of her husband Davey when Jo was fifteen and Stella only five had led her to a very low point. It had been up to Jo to be a mother to Stella until Maureen clawed her way back up to the light. Since then, both looked to Jo to make decisions.

'I'll go and speak to Gav,' she said. 'He might know where she's gone.'

'Unless he's gone with her,' Andy muttered.

Jo stood up. 'Now you're being ridiculous. Gav's fond of Stella, but not in that way.'

'Stella can't help being a man magnet. She turns heads. You probably can't understand that, but I'm not exaggerating. I'd be surprised if Gav's immune.'

'Thanks for the vote of confidence,' Jo said drily.

She wasn't too upset about Andy's comment. She was perfectly self-aware. Stella had inherited all the good looks, with her curly blonde hair and big blue eyes. Jo, on the other hand, could blend in anywhere, being of average height with shoulder-length brown hair and brown eyes.

'I didn't mean . . . You're very attractive too, just not like Stella. Or rather . . . ' Andy flushed as he tried to make amends.

Jo patted his back and went to the front door. 'Don't worry, no offence taken. I'll let you know when I find out where she is. Oh, and Andy . . . '

'Yes?'

'You don't need to worry about Gav whisking Stella away. He's in a longstanding engagement with someone else.'

Andy looked relieved as he waved Jo off. She headed back into the centre of the town. Gav's café occupied a strategic corner on the town centre square where there was a lot of footfall. Workers in nearby offices came in at lunchtime for sandwiches and hot pies, while there was a good trade all day in speciality flavoured coffees. Jo breathed in the delicious aromas of caramel latte and lemon drizzle cake as she pushed open the café entrance door.

Gav was serving behind the counter and Lizzie, his waitress, was wiping down tables and taking orders. She winked at Jo and continued with her busy tasks.

'What do you fancy?' Gav grinned at her. 'Lemon drizzle is hot out of the oven.'

'It's tempting, but I've just had lunch so I'd better not. I'll have a coffee, please; black, no sugar.'

'Coming right up, on the house.' Gav passed her a steaming, generously filled mug.

'Thanks. I was wondering if you'd seen Stella today?'

Gav raised an eyebrow. 'Not today. It's her day off. She hasn't, has she?'

Jo nodded. 'I'm afraid she has, yet again. I don't know why you keep her on. She's terribly unreliable.'

Gav laughed. 'Yeah, she is. Thank goodness I've got Lizzie. Truth is, I don't need a second waitress. This place is small enough, so Lizzie and I can cope fine. Stella's my act of charity. She reminds me of myself at that age, and how easy it is to go off the rails if there isn't some stability in your life.'

Jo knew Gav had had a bad childhood and rebellious teens and twenties. However, he had a strong, determined personality and had made something of himself. Was Stella able to do that? Sometimes Jo feared that her sister would fritter away her life. What would it take for her to find her way?

'You're very good to her,' Jo said, sipping her coffee. 'She's taken off again, and I don't know where's she gone.'

'No note?'

'Not this time. That's what's strange. Mum noticed her wardrobe was emptied and her suitcase was gone. She checked the kitchen table but there's no letter. That's where Stella usually leaves her notes.'

'I'm really sorry, but I haven't heard from her. But try not to worry; she'll pop up soon enough. Likely as not she'll message you.'

A couple came in and Jo stood back while they ordered at the counter. They dithered, changing their minds over what kind of cake to have. Jo tried not to feel impatient. She was conscious of Maureen waiting at home for news. Eventually the couple sat at a table and Lizzie took over two plates of meringues topped with thick cream.

'I'd better go soon,' she said. 'How are the wedding plans going?'

'Very well. Phil's happy with what we'll wear, and I've booked the cars and the photographer. You will come to the wedding? It's not until October. You and Stella and Maureen are all invited. And you can bring a significant other.' Gav smiled invitingly.

'I'm glad you and Phil finally agreed on a date for the wedding, and we'll all be there,' Jo said. 'You needn't bother with the significant other invite, though. I won't be bringing anyone.'

'It's four months away — plenty of time to find someone,' Gav shouted after her as she headed out onto the pavement.

Jo wasn't looking for romance; she had too many other things to focus on. For one, she had a big decision to make that was long overdue. She was planning on moving out into her own flat; it had taken three years but she'd saved up the deposit. So why was she hesitating? She could have left six months ago. But Jo knew she wasn't ready. She was scared of the unknown. While Stella flew butterfly-like at new situations, Jo was risk-averse to the extent that she was hiding from that next big step. Part of her longed for her own place, while the other part fretted about mortgages, independence and the possibility of loneliness.

A light rain began to fall. Jo shivered as a raindrop trickled down her neck. It was mid-June but it felt like mid-February. The sky was grey and it was chilly. Maureen was watching for her.

'Well?'

Jo shook her head. 'Andy doesn't

know where she's gone, nor does Gav.'

'It's so unlike her to leave without some kind of letter. Should we call the police?'

'It's too early for that. Stella's a twenty-year-old adult who's taken off under her own steam.'

'Or has she?' Maureen said darkly.

'Yes, Mum, she has. It's completely in character for her to vanish. I really don't think she's been kidnapped, and neither do you.' Jo kept her voice light but firm.

Maureen's eyes glistened. 'I don't know what I'd do without you, love, I don't. So what do we do now?'

'We check our phones for messages and we wait.'

'I need to do something or I'll go mad!'

'Okay, why don't we check Stella's room again? Maybe we've missed a clue.' Jo didn't think so, but it was puzzling. Even Stella wasn't usually selfish enough to rush away without an explanation.

Stella's bedroom was its usual explosion of colour and scent. There were clothes and makeup strewn everywhere. It was difficult to see whether anything was missing. For a girl who worked at a café a few days a week, she owned a lot of stuff. Jo suspected their mother was to blame. Maybe if she didn't shell out money, Stella would grow up and get a proper job and start paying her own way.

'Let's look at this with a fresh eye,' Jo said, more to herself than to Maureen. 'What's missing, what's out of place?'

'Her suitcase is gone, and half the clothes in her wardrobe,' Maureen said helpfully.

Jo rifled through the pretty dresses, the trousers and jumpers. A waft of flowery perfume tickled her nose. She was struck suddenly and powerfully by a sense of loss. Where was Stella? Jo had always protected her. When Stella was five and Maureen in mourning, Jo had made her little sister meals, dressed her for school and made sure she did her homework. She had pushed down her own grief at her father's death to concentrate on making sure Stella was all right. Later she'd struggled with the girl's terrible teenage years, which Maureen seemed unable to cope with. Jo and Stella had had some battles, but they'd come through, and remained good friends and loving sisters.

Jo scanned the room once more. 'Did you check under the bed?'

'I hardly think she's under there,' Maureen said.

Jo dropped to her knees and lifted the frilly cover; there was no harm in checking for clues. There was a shoebox there, its lid half off. Jo pulled it out. Perhaps it was nothing. She removed the lid. Inside was a small pile of postcards, which she recognised.

'What is it?' Maureen peered over her shoulder.

'It's my postcards from Max. Why has Stella got them?'

'I have no idea. Let me see. Goodness, there's letters too. They look like copies of what she's sent to him, but I don't see any replies.'

'Max only sends postcards, never letters.'

'These were all sent at Christmases past.'

'That's the only contact we have these days. We exchange Christmas cards — or, in his case, postcards.'

Max was Jo's pen-pal from primary school. When she was ten, her teacher arranged a correspondence with a German school class of the same age. Every pupil was given someone to write to, and Jo got Max. The letters to and fro were in English, as Jo hadn't learnt another language. The German pupils were learning English and glad to practise it. Long after Jo had moved to high school, she and Max were still writing. Only once the awkward later teenage years arrived had their correspondence dwindled. Then it was an exchange of Christmas greetings annually, which had continued over the years.

'Why is Stella writing to Max? He's my pen-pal.'

Maureen smiled. 'You sound about ten years old.'

Jo blushed. Yes, she did. It wasn't right to be possessive of Max. She'd never even met him. She remembered the long, heartfelt letters they used to write to each other. She'd poured all her youthful innermost thoughts and hopes and dreams into them. Max seemed to understand her better than the friends around her. At some fundamental level they had clicked.

'Stella used to send little messages and drawings to him in with your letters,' Maureen reminded her.

'That's true. But she was only a little kid then.'

'She worships you. That's why she used to copy you when she was small. Writing to Max was part of that.'

'So how do you explain these?' Jo spread out the copies. Each page was topped with 'Dear Max' and tailed with 'Love from Stella'. The dates were recent, starting in January and ending at the beginning of June.

'I don't know,' Maureen said, picking them up to read. 'Why is she writing to a stranger when she has Andy to confide in?'

Max isn't a stranger, Jo wanted to say.

'I wonder if he answered her letters. I don't see any cards from him.' Maureen rummaged in the shoebox.

'She sent him her mobile phone number,' Jo said, glancing at the letters. 'Maybe he messages her instead. After all, writing snail-mail is so old-fashioned.' She tried to swallow her jealousy. She was being ridiculous.

'What did Andy have to say?' Maureen asked, taking the letters and closing the box on them.

Jo stared at the shoe box as if it had answers. 'He asked her to marry him.'

'What a daft man he is.' Maureen rolled her eyes. 'He might love her, but he doesn't know her awfully well if he thought that was a good idea.' They shared a smile. 'Come on, love, let's have a cup of tea and see if that helps us think where the minx has gone.'

'Wait, Mum — where's Stella's passport?' Jo said as a sudden dreadful thought popped into her head.

'It's in this drawer here, with her birth certificate and other documents.' Maureen pulled open the top drawer in Stella's writing desk and gasped. 'Jo, it's not here. It's gone.'

Jo, not a bit surprised now, went over and looked at the contents of the drawer. There was an unsealed envelope half-hidden under a powder compact. Stella appeared to use the space for important pieces of paper and also for face powder, mascara and partially empty bottles of nail varnish. 'She must've written this in a hurry and forgotten to leave it out on the kitchen table.' The message was short and scribbled, so that Jo could hardly read it. 'She says she has to get away for a while. She's going to visit Max in Germany.'

'Give me that.' Maureen snatched it from her and frowned as if she could make the words tell a different story. Then she sat heavily on the bed, her hand to her mouth.

'It's all right, Mum,' Jo soothed. 'She'll come home in a few days. I bet she won't even get on the plane. Besides, how has she got enough cash for an airline ticket to Germany?'

Maureen gave a groan.

'Oh Mum, you didn't give her more money?'

'She's not sensible like you. You've got a steady career; your own business. Stella makes a pittance at that café.'

Jo bit back a retort that Stella was young, healthy, intelligent, and quite capable of finding a decent job or going to college to train for her own career.

'There's only one solution,' Maureen said, raising worried eyes to Jo. 'You'll have to go after her and bring her home.'

2

Jo stepped out of the aeroplane at Basle into searing heat. She felt the sun burn her hair and quickly put on her sun hat. It was a marked contrast to the miserable English summer she'd left behind. The temperature in Switzerland was twenty-nine degrees Celsius, and the forecast in southern Germany even hotter.

Her heart thumped as she checked her bag for her passport for what felt like the millionth time. She wasn't used to travelling abroad. She had gone on two package holidays. Once, when she was twenty-five and earning her first decent salary from her business start-up, she'd gone for a week to Turkey. Although she'd enjoyed the warm turquoise sea and the ancient ruins, she'd suffered from the heat and had a horrible bout of food poisoning, and had been relieved to return home. Her second package had been last year, when she'd treated the family to a fortnight in Tenerife. That had been lovely. Jo smiled at the memories. Maureen had loved sunbathing on the beach, while Stella wandered the markets buying cheap jewellery and ethnic cotton skirts. It had been easy travel. Jo had handed over the money and the travel agent did the rest. It had been an all-inclusive package, which meant their guide took charge the minute their plane landed until she waved them off fourteen days later on their return flight.

Jo's situation now was quite different. She'd booked a flight herself on the internet from London to Basle, and then had to work out the train timetables to get from Switzerland to Germany and the tiny village that Max lived in. He lived in a place called the Kaiserstuhl. This translated as 'The Emperor's Chair', Jo's guidebook, hastily purchased, informed her. It was a region of hills overlooking the Rhine Valley, where rich volcanic soils supported vineyards and picturesque villages.

Which all sounded delightful if one had a human guide. As it was, Jo nervously followed the other passengers through security and the inevitable passport checks, and then found herself outside where there were buses, taxis and cars and lots of people milling about.

In the end it had taken Jo a week to leave England, despite Maureen's urging to hurry up and go. Jo had clients to meet and loose ends to tie up before she could travel. When she'd gone to Andy and explained the situation, he had cried and told her to please bring Stella home. If she didn't want to get married, that was okay by him. He wouldn't mention the topic again. Jo then went to Gav, who laughed when he heard where Stella was. Good luck to her, he said, and could she please bring back some fine

German wines for the wedding on her return?

'You do realise this isn't ideal for me?' Jo said to Maureen as she packed her suitcase.

'But you can work anywhere, can't you?' Maureen said, looking anxious as if Jo would refuse to go. 'Stella needs you. She's confused, and you're the only one who can talk her through this.'

'We don't actually know what's going through Stella's head,' Jo said.

'Well, whatever it is, she'll need you,' Maureen said firmly.

And that was that. Jo gazed out the window as the train drew into the village. It really was lovely, with old houses all topped with red tiles and the spire of a church in the background. Beyond were the hazy outlines of the hills. She stepped off the train, patting her pockets to check she had everything. She pulled out her map and tried to work out where she was and where Max's house was. She knew his address was Eisen Schloss. There it was on the map; it was marked just outside the village.

Ten minutes' walk later, Jo realised why Max's house was singled out on the map. She stood on the cobbled street and craned her neck to look up at the castle nestled into the hillside above her. A tiny winding path led up to it. She wiped her forehead, feeling damp and sweaty. If only she'd been able to freshen up. She wanted to meet Max looking clean and smelling fragrant. But then again, why did it matter so much? She was here to apologise for her sister, and they wouldn't be staying for long.

Had Max ever mentioned living in a castle? She thought not. He'd written about his family home and how much he loved it. He'd described the view from his bedroom in one of his first letters to her. Perhaps he had lived somewhere else before. After all, what did she really know about Max as a grown man?

There was an odd sensation in her

stomach. It was going to be strange, finally seeing him. He had been such a comforting part of her life for the last twenty years. She looked forward to his Christmas postcard, and she'd kept all the letters he'd written her during their school years. Now she was suddenly unsure about him. Would it spoil everything if they finally met? Like watching the film of a book you loved and being disappointed with the actors, who were nothing like what you'd imagined the characters to be?

Anyway, there was no way round it, Jo reminded herself. Stella was up there somewhere. It was Jo's duty to go and find her. She took a last glance at the castle before heading to the path. It wasn't large, but it had a certain charm. Made of honey-coloured stone, with crenellated turrets and a wide terrace, it seemed almost to float above a massed thicket of green shrubs and pink dog rose.

'Like Sleeping Beauty's castle,' Jo murmured, then shook her head at her whimsy. The heat was getting to her. It certainly made her walk slowly up the path. She was almost panting by the time she reached the top. She fumbled in her bag for a bottle of water and drank gratefully.

She walked in through two tall gateposts topped with stone lions. The driveway was neat with honey-coloured chippings and tidy flower beds. There were no cars and no sign of anybody. No one answered the door at her three-ring press of the bell. Jo stood there, undecided. Would it be rude to go round the back? She hesitated. She had a room booked in the only guest house in the village. The place clearly wasn't on the usual tourist route. Perhaps she ought to go back down and book in. She could freshen up and then come back later in the cool of the evening to find Stella.

Or . . . she could have a quick peek round the other side of the castle. Surely it would do no harm? Her feet were already walking as she mulled over the options. The sweet scent of roses wafted in the warm air towards her. Her skin was brushed by the soft leaves as she went by. Then there were three broad, shallow stairs leading up onto the terrace she'd spied from below.

'Jo! Oh my goodness. Am I seeing things? Jo, what are you doing here?' Stella's voice shrieked over the fronds of a palm.

Jo was enveloped in a tight hug which nearly toppled her from the top stair. She hugged her sister back just as fiercely, as relief coursed through her. Thank goodness, she'd found her. It was one thing knowing that Stella had come to see Max, but quite another to actually see her. Stella's favourite perfume trailed them both. It took Jo back instantly to the moment she'd rummaged in the wardrobe, missing her sister like mad. She started to laugh, and Stella joined in.

'OMG, I can't believe this,' Stella said, wiping her eyes and dragging Jo onto the terrace. There were two sun loungers there, along with a white-painted wrought-iron table and chairs. 'Come and see this — isn't it marvellous? I had no idea Max owned a whole blooming castle. This terrace is where I practically live. Look at that view over the village and the whole Kaiserstuhl. Isn't it fab?'

For a moment, Stella's enthusiasm flowed into Jo too. They might have been on holiday, exclaiming at their accommodation and the new country to explore. Then she was only too aware that Stella had let people down, and they were standing in the grounds of a man whom neither of them really knew.

'Can we sit down?' Jo asked, feeling slightly faint.

'You take that lounger. I've got my book on this one.'

'No, let's . . . let's sit at the table. We need to talk.' There was no way Jo could talk sense into Stella if they were lying down sunbathing.

'Not now, please,' Stella said. 'Can't we just enjoy the moment? Max isn't here; he had to go into the city for business. He'll be back later. We can talk then.'

'I'd rather talk to you now, before Max gets back. What I have to say isn't for others people's ears.'

' You're always so serious,' Stella complained. 'I'm really not up for this. I don't have to listen to you.'

'I think you do. I think you owe me that courtesy, as I've travelled a long way to find you.'

Stella snorted rudely. 'I didn't ask you to. This is my life, Jo, not yours.'

'It becomes mine when you upset Mum and make Andy cry and let Gav down.'

There was a sudden silence between them. Jo made a conscious effort to relax. It wouldn't do any good to have a blazing argument with her sister.

'Andy cried?' Stella sounded upset now.

'He's fine. He wants you to go home. And if you don't want to get married, he won't mention it again.'

'He told you what happened, then.'

'Yes, I got the whole story. He's a lovely man, Stella, and I don't know how you can treat him like this. Did you have to run away? Couldn't you discuss it with him?'

Stella tossed back her thick mane of hair and wrinkled her perfect nose. 'Sometimes Andy is *too* lovely.'

'What on earth does that mean? Honestly, you are your own worst enemy. You and Andy are made for each other.'

'That's just it,' Stella said, finally meeting Jo's gaze. 'I don't know if we are. I mean, Andy's great and he'll make a good husband — but will I ever make a good wife? I got scared and I ran. It's what I do. Yes, I know what you're going to say; that I should stay and sort it all out. But I can't. I need some space to think about what I want to do.'

'You're rather young to get married, but at least be honest with him and talk it through. As for Mum, she's really upset that you've gone.'

Stella chewed one of her nails. 'I left a note.'

'Yes, thank you, we did find it eventually,' Jo said.

'I left it on the table, didn't I? I meant to.'

'It doesn't matter. What matters is that I'm here to take you home.'

Stella looked horrified. 'I'm not going home.'

'You can't stay here taking advantage of Max's good nature.'

'Why not? He's told me I'm welcome to stay as long as I need to.'

'And that's another thing.' Jo stood up as a slight irritation stirred. 'Why were you writing to Max this year?'

Stella's eyes followed her as she paced on the beautiful paved floor. It was like a Roman mosaic, with blue and white chips patterning the ochre tiles.

'Well?' Jo prompted when Stella didn't speak.

'I don't know. Andy and I weren't

getting along for a while and I needed someone to talk to.'

Jo was hurt. 'Why didn't you speak to me? I'm always there for you.'

'You'd have told me what a wonderful guy Andy is and how I ought to feel lucky having him.'

Jo opened her mouth and then closed it again. Stella was right; that was exactly what she'd have said. It was uncomfortable to be so predictable. 'Why Max?' she asked. 'What about your friends?'

'I suppose I wanted someone who wasn't involved at all.' Stella poured two glasses of water from a jug on the table and offered one to Jo. 'I found your postcard stash when I was borrowing your amethyst earrings just after Christmas, and on impulse I wrote to Max. At first he didn't write back, but I kept writing and I sent him my mobile number. After a while, he texted me.'

'And he told you to come here and visit?'

'Not exactly.' Stella studied her drink and mopped up a single water drop as it slid down the outside of the glass.

'What happened?'

'I asked him if I could come here,' Stella said. 'He didn't answer immediately, but then he texted me and said if I needed help, I could come and stay. He did say if I was in any kind of trouble that I should confide in you.'

That warmed Jo's heart. Max had thought of her. He hadn't persuaded Stella to come to Germany; in fact he'd tried to stop her. She looked at her sister. Stella didn't wilt in the heat like Jo. She looked fresh and pretty in her white sundress and buttercup-yellow sandals, her hair sun-bleached to the lightest shade of blonde. Her blue eyes were startling against her tanned face. How could Max resist her? Without having met him, Jo was disappointed in him all of a sudden.

'I don't want to go home,' Stella said in a small voice. 'Please, Jo, just a few more days? I'm sure Max will let you stay here too.'

'What about Mum?' Jo said. 'At the very least you need to phone her and tell her you're okay.'

She'd lost the argument. Stella wanted to be here. Max wanted Stella to be here. Who was Jo to tell them otherwise? A few days wouldn't matter. She had her laptop, and plenty of work she could do from here, assuming Max had a good internet connection.

Stella shrieked and leapt up to hug Jo. 'Thank you, thank you. I'll phone Mum right now. We'll have such fun here, I promise you. Oh Jo, I'm so glad you came to find me. This is simply fabulous.'

'It's only a couple of days, and then we're going back home,' Jo warned.

But Stella had stopped listening. She grabbed Jo's hand excitedly. 'Come on — there's something I want to show you right now.'

Jo followed her round to the back of the building. Her first impression was of intensely green lawns. Sprinklers were on, keeping the grass healthy. There was a small parterre and a patio fringed with hibiscus. But Stella wasn't interested in that. She pointed with a wide grin.

'Guess what that is.'

There was a double patio door, made in top-to-bottom glass, currently pushed wide open. Inside was a scene of mayhem. A cloud of plaster dust billowed out towards them. There was shouting in German and the high-pitched whine of a drill.

'I have no idea. Max is renovating his kitchen?' Jo hazarded a guess.

Stella shook her head impatiently. 'Much more exciting than that. Come on!'

'I'd rather you just told me.'

'Oh, you're no fun.'

'Honestly, I'm hot and tired and I need to book into my guest house, so whatever it is, please just spit it out.'

Stella made a face at her. 'Well, since you're going to be a bore, I'll tell you.

Max opens up some of the rooms in the castle to visitors because it has quite a history, apparently.'

'I wouldn't have thought there were enough tourists to make it worthwhile,' Jo said. 'There are hardly any rooms in the village, and I couldn't see any mention of a tourist information place when I searched the web.'

'I don't know about that, but anyway, that's not what's so exciting. See all the work going on? Max is opening a small tea room. Remember Mum and Dad's café?'

There was such longing in Stella's voice. All the memories flooded back to Jo in a swirl of joy and sadness. Their parents had owned a small restaurant before Dad got sick. Stella called it a café, but it had been more than that. It had started a bit like Gav's café, but was so successful that Maureen and Davey had then served lunches and evening meals. They had bought the neighbouring premises and knocked through, creating a bigger space.

'You were so small; how can you remember much about it?' Jo said.

'It's just snatches of good smells and laughter. I remember Dad lifting me up to get the glasses down from the shelf and Mum letting me stir the cake mix in the pan. I remember being happy.'

'There were red and white checked tablecloths and a candle at each table,' Jo added with a smile. 'I was allowed to light the candles for the dinner sittings. I was so proud of myself. You used to follow me about and beg to light one, but you were too small. The customers loved to see you. Mum was the chef and Dad did all the business side of things. But he was also the life and soul of the place, making sure everyone was contented; that the food was to their satisfaction and that they were pleased and would come back.'

'He loved to talk,' Stella said. 'I do remember that. Sometimes I have to grab onto my memories of him, or I'm afraid they'll fade.'

Jo reached out and squeezed her

sister's hand. Their lives had come crashing down when their father died. Maureen had sold the restaurant and retreated into herself. All their happiness had evaporated, and after that it had been a struggle for so long. Jo hoped it hadn't felt like a struggle for Stella. She'd protected her as much as possible.

A workman in plaster-coated overalls came out. His face split into a wide grin when he saw Stella. He was in his twenties, tall and thin with dark hair.

'Hey, how are you today?' His English was good, with a strong local accent.

'Jo, this is Uwe. He works for Max — usually in the vineyards, but he's helping to build the tea room. Uwe, this is my sister.'

Uwe shook Jo's hand politely, but his attention was all on Stella. Jo watched her sister giggle at his jokes and wondered if she had mentioned Andy at all. She rather thought not.

'I'm going out tonight with Uwe and

some of his mates to a party in the village,' Stella said as Uwe waved a casual hand and went back inside. 'You could come along if you want.'

'It's a kind invitation, but you don't want your elderly sister cramping your style. I'll probably wait and meet Max and then have a quiet evening in the guest house.'

Stella glanced beyond Jo and smiled. 'You won't have to wait. Here's Max coming now.'

Jo's heart lurched weirdly as she turned around. Max had grown into a tall man with broad shoulders. She recognised the boy's features in the adult; they had exchanged photos as children. His grey eyes and dark blond hair were the same, except the softness of the boy was now replaced with a strong jaw and muscled frame. As he reached her, she saw he looked tired, and there was a sadness in his eyes not quite hidden as he smiled in welcome.

'Hello, Jo.' His English was perfect, without accent.

'Max.' She didn't know what to say. How to encompass twenty years of long-distance friendship into one initial greeting?

'You look the same as when you were ten years old.' Max smiled.

'I'm not sure whether to be flattered by that or not. I'd have recognised you, too.'

'It's wonderful that you're here. Please . . . come in out of the heat so we can talk properly.'

He led the way to a side door, away from the noise of hammering and drilling. Inside, Jo felt immediately the cool peace of Max's home.

'When did you arrive?' Max asked politely.

'Just about an hour ago,' Jo replied. 'I'm staying at the Gasthof Villengen. Do you know it?'

'Yes, of course. It's a small village, and everyone knows everyone else's business, I'm afraid. The guest house is fine, but you must stay here with Stella instead.'

'I couldn't possibly put you out like that.'

Their conversation was so mundane. Yet what had she expected? They were hardly going to have the same intense emotional exchanges that they'd had as ten-year-olds all those years ago. They were exactly what they now appeared: two acquaintances making mannerly conversation.

'Please, Jo? There's plenty of room here, and I will enjoy the company. You must stay as long as you like. There's no rush.'

Again she saw a brief shadow cross his gaze before he turned away from her. Max, the boy she had known so well, had grown into a handsome man. Jo realised she didn't know him at all.

3

The workmen had gone home, and Jo was upstairs having a lie-down before dinner. Max couldn't quite believe she was here. The pretty girl he remembered from the photos she'd sent him had turned into a lovely, if rather solemn, woman. He had finally persuaded her that it was no problem to stay at the castle. In the end he'd rather forced the issue by phoning the Gasthof Villengen and explaining the situation to Frau Bauer. She was an old friend of his mother's and was not at all put out by losing her guest.

'This is good for you,' she told him. 'This is what you need to take your mind off your troubles.'

Max had turned the conversation to other things, asking after her husband's health and the state of their vegetable plot. He'd no intention of discussing his problems even with this kindly woman.

He frowned. His visit to Freiburg, the nearest city, had solved nothing. Franz Stoller was an old friend as well as Max's lawyer, and his advice had been to try to force the issue with Sylvie by threatening legal action. Max had declined, however. He had enjoyed lunch with Franz and made his escape. No, he'd work this through without a lawyer, even if it all seemed impossible right now.

Stella came bouncing up the steps towards him. 'Is Jo still asleep? Will you pass her a message from me?'

She looked full of energy. She was dressed in a pale blue shift dress and strappy sandals, which made her tanned skin glow. A pair of large sunglasses, pushed high on her head, held back her thick blonde hair. She had a tiny bag with her that she swung with one hand while waiting for Max's response.

He wondered if he'd done the right thing in letting Stella come to stay with him. She had been very persistent with her letters. At first he hadn't answered them. Partially, he was too busy with the vineyards and developing tourism at the castle. Mostly, he felt uncomfortable being the recipient of such intimate correspondence. He had advised her to speak to Jo, but when she pleaded with him for a place to stay, he'd given in. Space was no problem at Eisen Schloss. He had been planning to contact Jo about her sister when she, too, arrived on his doorstep.

'What's the message?' he asked now.

'I'm going into the village to meet Uwe. I'll be back late. It's just that Jo's a worrier, and I don't want her fretting and checking the time all night. Remind her I'm twenty, will you?' She leaned over and gave him a peck on the cheek.

'I'll let her know,' he said. 'Enjoy yourself — but take care, okay? Make sure Uwe escorts you back.'

She rolled her eyes. 'You're worse than her.' She turned and skipped back down the steps without a backwards glance.

Max smiled to himself. What it was to be twenty. Stella struck him as young for her age. He thought of Petra and the smile slid from his lips. He should be giving her advice, and she should be rolling her teenage eyes in exasperation. Max gave a sigh that lifted his shoulders. It was true how the saying went: you couldn't outrun your troubles.

'Max?'

He turned at Jo's soft voice. She stood uncertainly in the shadow of the hallway. Her dark brown hair was slightly curled where she'd lain on it, and her eyes were sleepy. She rubbed at them and yawned.

'You don't have to get up,' he said. 'You can go back to bed and have supper later.'

'No, no, I don't want to waste the evening,' she said, shaking her head. 'I'm finding it hard to wake up, but give me a minute.'

'If you manage to wake up, you can join me for some dinner. I'm not a great cook, but I can rustle up some wienerschnitzel and green salad.'

'And there, I was just about to say how good your English is when you throw in a German word. What is a veener . . . whatsit?'

'My mother was English, so I grew up speaking both languages. You don't remember that?'

'Actually I do, now you've reminded me,' Jo said. 'Gosh, I'd forgotten. That's why you wanted to have an English pen-pal, wasn't it? To help with idioms and the culture, so you could chat to your mum in her own language.'

'That's right. I was so happy when you wrote back to me. My very own English friend, who would write ten pages of lovely words for me each week to devour.'

Jo laughed. 'Yeah, I really did, didn't I? I poured my heart out in those letters. I hope you threw them out; they'd be so embarrassing to read now.'

'I haven't thrown them out. I've still got every single letter you ever sent me.'

Jo took in a breath. 'Wow.'

'So you threw my letters out?' Max couldn't help asking in return.

Her eyes were almond-coloured, he decided. Not as dark as chocolate, but deeper brown than hazel. Their colour wasn't clear in the old battered photo of the young Jo, but he saw them now perfectly against her pale skin.

'No, I've got all your letters and your postcards too. I wouldn't dream of getting rid of them.'

They smiled at each other. Max's breath caught in his throat for a brief moment. 'Right,' he finally said, clapping his hands and stepping back, 'wienerschnitzel it is for dinner. It's a local speciality of breaded meat fried in a pan. You'll find it quite delicious. Do you drink wine?'

Jo visibly jumped at his sudden loud energy. 'Wine . . . yes, thank you, I do drink it. I'm looking forward to the meat and . . . can I help? Can I make the salad?'

Max relaxed. They were onto safe subjects now. Food and drink. After dinner he'd show her around the castle like a tourist. They might have opened their hearts to each other as kids, but that didn't mean they had anything in common as adults. He wasn't good at small talk. Mostly he kept his own company and didn't have to talk at all. He was content with a book or newspaper. Stella had rather disturbed this habit by chatting to him in the evenings. Now there was Jo.

'Before I forget,' he said, 'Stella asked me to tell you she's away to a party with Uwe and she'll be back late. She doesn't want you to worry about her.'

Jo raised her eyebrows. 'If she didn't want me to worry, she shouldn't have left home.'

Max leaned back on the sideboard and folded his arms. 'Want to tell me what's going on?'

Jo tried not to notice how muscular his arms were or how his dark blond hair curled slightly, catching the evening light. His long legs stretched out before him as he leaned there. With a shock she realised she found him very attractive. It was an unusual sensation, and it rippled pleasantly over her skin. It was a long while since she'd been attracted to someone. There was no harm in it, she thought quickly. Max didn't have to know.

Now it was his turn to raise his brows in query. She realised he was waiting for an answer. 'Stella hasn't told you why she's here?' she countered with her own question.

'Some unhappiness with her boy-friend, I presume from reading her letters. It wasn't very clear what exactly was the problem with him.'

'There isn't a problem with Andy,' Jo said. 'The problem is all with Stella.'

'I thought maybe he was abusive.'

Jo laughed out loud; she couldn't help it. She saw Max's surprise and then his lips turning up into a smile at her merriment. She wiped at her eyes and took a breath. 'Andy is a lovely guy and he's far too good for my little sister,' she said. 'He'd never lift a finger to hurt her. He's so kind-hearted he carries spiders outside when he finds them in the house, or so Stella tells me.'

'So what's this fellow done to make Stella run five hundred miles to Germany?'

'Believe it or not, he wants to marry her. My sister got frightened and ran away. It's what she does when she doesn't want to confront her emotions.'

'Was it a mistake, letting her stay here?' Max asked, sounding genuinely concerned.

'No, it was incredibly good of you to take her in. She seems really happy here.'

'But you want her to go back?'

'Yes, I do. I think she owes it to Andy to talk to him face to face like an adult.'

'She's young for her age,' Max said, echoing his thoughts from earlier.

Jo nodded. 'She is that. It's my fault. I pretty much brought her up when our mother was ill. I should've let her make her own mistakes more often. I'm afraid I mollycoddled her instead.'

'It's not an easy task, bringing up a child.' For a moment Max's face tightened, then he gave Jo a brief smile. 'Shall we go and make our dinner?'

Somehow she'd hit a nerve, she was sure of it. But she didn't like to ask Max what she'd said to make him change the conversation so abruptly. Instead, she took her cue from him and followed him into a huge open-plan kitchen quite at odds with the ancient exterior of the castle.

'Do you like it?' he asked.

'It's wonderful, but do you need so much space to cook?'

'I renovated it recently, thinking ahead to the café opening up. It will be a back-up for the café kitchen in case that oven breaks down and we need to bake for customers.'

'Of course. I hadn't thought of that. Will you be doing the baking yourself?' Jo couldn't quite imagine him with an apron on, pulling trays of cupcakes from the ovens.

'No. I think I told you, I'm not a great cook. I'll hire staff to run the café for me. I'm too busy with the vineyards. This is simply a side venture. I'll see how it does.'

Jo wished she had as much confidence as Max. He was running businesses from the castle with not a nerve in sight, while she couldn't even manage to buy her own flat.

'So you want to take Stella home?' he said as he put a pan on one of the huge cooker tops and moved to a tall fridge to fetch meat and vegetables.

'If I had my way, we'd be off to the plane tomorrow,' Jo said. 'Mum is desperate for me to get Stella home. But I've agreed we can stay for a couple of days longer. That is, if you don't mind?'

'Take as long as you wish,' he said, putting a curl of butter onto the hot frying pan. 'The castle is roomy, and I'm hardly ever here. Please treat the place as your own home.'

Jo's heart sank a little. If Max was hardly here, she wouldn't get a chance to get to know him. Still, she had to remember that he hadn't initiated their meeting; it had been forced upon him by Stella's selfishness. Probably Max would rather never have met her. After all, it wasn't as if they were more than casual correspondents nowadays.

She didn't feel hungry anymore.

* * *

The music was loud and the reverberations thumped through Stella's head. She swigged down her third glass of wine and felt thirsty. Hot bodies moved around her as people danced and swayed to the song. Uwe waved to her with a bottle, and she nodded with a smile. Why not? Here she was in Germany, having a great time at a party. If she wanted another glass of wine, who was going to stop her? Not Andy, that was for sure. She was free to make her own decisions.

She didn't want to think about Andy. If she did, his sad face would float in front of her eyes, filled with the pain of rejection. If only he hadn't bought her a ring. It was a very nice ring, too: an old gold band with a single beautiful diamond sparkling on top. Briefly she'd imagined her slender finger with the ring on and her friends all admiring it. Then reality had hit hard. She didn't want to get married. She was too young to settle down. Andy's love was suddenly cloying, like being wrapped in a warm, humid blanket. So Stella had done what she did best: she ran.

On the plane, she'd rationalised that she needed space to make a decision. It made perfect sense to go to Max. He'd said she could stay with him. Okay, he hadn't been a great communicator, not answering her letters; but hey, he was there and he had a place for her to stay.

Maybe she'd carry on living in Germany, she mused, swaying to the beat of a song she liked. She'd get a job in a bar and hang out all summer. The only fly in the ointment was Jo turning up. A couple of days' grace, then Jo wanted them to go home. Stella remembered she'd promised Jo to phone their mother. It was too noisy at the party. She decided she'd phone in the morning.

'Stella, you want this?' Uwe shouted, pushing a glass full of wine at her. It slopped onto her dress and she shrieked.

'Sorry.' He grinned, not looking sorry at all. Someone shouted in German behind him and he turned and called back. Stella had not one clue what he or anyone else was saying. He swung back round to her and tried to kiss her. Stella pushed him away.

'You're drunk,' she said.

'You're gorgeous. Let's dance.' He started moving about in a jerky fashion.

Stella had no option but to keep dancing or to push her way forcefully through the throng. She was having a good time, she reminded herself. She and Andy hardly ever went to parties. Which was wrong. She was twenty, not forty, and she deserved to have some fun. With renewed energy, she gave Uwe a wide smile and then began to dance in earnest.

* * *

Back at the castle, Jo and Max sat outside on the terrace in the sultry night air. It smelt of warm earth, lush vines and melted candle wax. Between them, on the white-painted wrought-iron table, were the remains of their meal: plates with scraps of breaded meat, the last shreds of lettuce, and dishes with just a smear of berries from the excellent raspberry cheesecake Max had served up as dessert.

'I'll never eat again,' Jo groaned, rubbing her stomach.

'You have a hearty appetite,' Max laughed.

'Which, translated in either German or English, means I'm a greedy pig.'

'I wouldn't be so rude as to say that.'

'But you're thinking it, I can see that.'

My goodness, was she flirting with Max? Somehow Jo didn't care. It felt good. The whole evening had been fun. Any awkwardness between them had vanished. They hadn't discussed any deep topics, Max carefully keeping to neutral things like cooking and German culture and describing the surrounding countryside. Jo had persuaded him to explain about the wine growing in the region and about the Eisen vineyards, or *reben* as he called them. It was interesting, and Max was good company once he loosened up. There was a reserve to him that needed breaching, and Jo noticed once or twice the sadness in his eyes when he gazed out over the terrace to the views beyond and didn't realise she was watching him.

He sat up straight. 'Well, thank you for a very nice evening, but I must head to bed. I've an early business meeting tomorrow. You know where your room is, and you must help yourself to whatever you need as if this were your home.'

'Yes, I've enjoyed this evening,' Jo said. 'Thanks for getting my bags from the guest house. Mrs Bauer didn't seem too unhappy to lose me.'

Max grinned. 'She knows you are in good hands here. Good night, Jo.'

'Good night, Max.' She watched his tall figure as he headed inside. The candles were almost burned down, and she sat there and decided she'd wait for Stella.

The candles were mere stubs when she heard a clattering on the steps behind her, followed by cursing. Swinging round, Jo saw Stella stumbling up the top step. Her hair was tumbling around her face and there was a red wine stain on her blue dress. She was barefoot and her sandals drooped from one hand.

'Shush!' Jo whispered fiercely as Stella loudly greeted her. 'Max has gone to bed.'

'Alone?' Stella leered.

'Oh, for goodness sake, you're totally wellied. Come and have a glass of water to sober you up,' Jo snapped.

'No, honestly . . . you and Max . . . you . . . Max . . . ' Stella slumped into the chair recently vacated by their host, put her head back and began to snore.

Jo shook her sister hard. Stella moaned. Jo shook her some more. Stella woke up.

'Wha . . . what? Ow, you're hurting me.'

'Oh Stella, what on earth kind of party was it? Did Uwe walk you back?'

Stella frowned as if concentrating. 'Yeah, he did . . . well, I think so. I'm here, aren't I?'

'It's this kind of behaviour that has to stop. Don't you see that?'

Stella waved a vague hand in front of Jo's face. 'You're so stuffy, that's your problem. You're thirty years old and you act like you're fifty.' She sat up, shaking her finger at Jo and becoming quite animated. 'I'm not the one with a problem, Jo. It's you. You're old before your time. How often do you have a laugh? Never, that's what. You're so serious, it's no wonder Max has gone to bed alone. And another thing . . . '

Her head fell forward and the snores rang out. Jo managed to get her sister up out of the chair and up the stairs to her bedroom. She didn't bother trying to get Stella into her nightie; she simply covered her with the duvet. For a moment she stood looking at her. Tenderly, she stroked a curl of blonde hair from Stella's mouth until it fell into place on the pillow.

Only too conscious of the silence in the castle, Jo made her way quietly to her own bedroom. Max had offered her the choice of two rooms. One was the blue room, which was very pretty, with a view to the gardens and vegetable field and had light blue walls and a dark blue ceiling. But Jo was smitten with the second choice. The room was smaller, but had a sloped ceiling and a fireplace and dark yellow walls. The bed had a buttercup-yellow duvet and pillows with tiny yellow flowers on a white background, and there was a dresser complete with a ceramic jug and bowl. Besides all that, the view was spectacular; it looked out onto the village below with the dark mountains as a backdrop.

Now she lay gratefully in the unfamiliar bed, wrestling with the heat of the night. She wore her thinnest nightie and still felt too hot. Stella's words stung in her ears: *You're old before your time. You never have a laugh.* The saddest part of it was knowing that Stella was right.

4

Jo woke in the morning with a sense of unease. It took her a moment to realise where she was. She stared at the unfamiliar yellow slanted ceiling. Then her heart lifted in pleasure — she was in Germany, in Max's castle. Like a small rollercoaster, her mood then plummeted. Stella's words came back to her.

With a sigh, Jo swung her legs out of bed. Her sister had a point: she was too serious. But there was a reason for that. She'd had a lot of responsibility for a long number of years. Looking after her baby sister had made her grow up fast. Having a laugh, as Stella put it, was way at the bottom of Jo's list of things to do. She was so busy nowadays, worrying about her mother and building up her own small business, that she rarely socialised and never really felt relaxed.

Jo paused in the act of gathering up a towel and toiletries. In fact, the most relaxed she'd been in ages was last night on Max's terrace, having dinner with him.

Trying not to read too much into that, she padded down the hall to the guest bathroom. Half an hour later, freshly showered and dressed in a cotton shirt and denim shorts, she went downstairs. Max was at his business meeting, she was sure, but he had said there'd be breakfast. Glancing at her watch, Jo reckoned it was unlikely that Stella would surface before lunch. As it was, it was only nine a.m.

She got a shock when she went into the vast kitchen. An older woman was bustling about, and there was the aroma of cooked eggs and warm pastry. Jo hadn't expected anyone to be there. Outside she heard the sound of a truck's engine and shouts. The workmen had arrived. She wondered if Uwe was there, and what state he was in after the party.

'Guten Morgen. Möchten Sie Frühstück?' The woman smiled at her.

'I'm sorry, I don't speak German.'

'I will try my rusty English. I'm Frau Hiss, Max's housekeeper. And you are Jo? Max has left me a message to say you are staying here as a guest and will need breakfast.'

'Your English isn't rusty at all,' Jo said, smiling back. 'It puts me to shame. I can't speak any foreign languages at all apart from a bit of schoolgirl French. Yes please to breakfast. Can I help you?'

Frau Hiss flapped her hands. 'No, you take a seat there and I'll bring you some eggs and croissants.'

'Silly of me, but I didn't think of Max having a housekeeper. Does he have other staff too?'

Frau Hiss lifted a tray and brought it over to the table. There were two soft-boiled eggs in pretty blue china eggcups and a plate with flaky croissants. She set down a pat of butter and a bowl of strawberry jam with it. The thoughtfulness of it all hit Jo. It was the little extra touches, such as the carefully folded napkin and the tiny spoon for the jam, that Frau Hiss had taken the trouble to add. Had Max told her to do so?

'It's a big property,' the housekeeper said. 'There are the vineyard workers, of course, and Max takes on seasonal people when it's harvest. For the house, it's just me. I think it'd be easier if I lived in, but he won't do that. He likes his space. So I come up from the village three days a week in the mornings, and clean and tidy and make some meals.'

'I haven't seen the rest of the castle yet,' Jo said, taking a bite of a delicious croissant.

'You can have a look after breakfast, but maybe Max can better show you about.'

'I need to work this morning anyway.' She'd brought her laptop, after all, and her clients wouldn't wait while she had an impromptu holiday.

'Shall I make breakfast for Stella?'

'I don't think she'll be awake yet. She can make her own breakfast later.'

Frau Hiss nodded. 'It's nice for Max. Perhaps it's a new start for him. She's a lovely young woman.'

'It's not . . . ' *It's not like that,* Jo wanted to say. What held her back was a tiny slice of uncertainty. It didn't *seem* as if Max and Stella had any romantic thoughts about each other, but she didn't say anything further.

Oblivious to Jo's confusion, Frau Hiss went on. 'It's good. It takes his mind off his daughter, I'm sure.' She picked up a pail and mop and went out of the kitchen, leaving Jo stunned.

So Max had a daughter. Why hadn't he mentioned her? And did that mean he also had a wife? In which case, where was she? And what did Frau Hiss mean by Max needing to have his mind taken off his daughter? It was too much to take in. Jo quickly finished her breakfast and washed up the plates. It wasn't her business. Although the information disquieted her, it really had nothing to do with her. She was here simply to take Stella home.

Yet she couldn't stop thinking about it as she started up her laptop, intending to work. It took all her determination to focus on her emails. There were rather a lot of them, as she hadn't looked at her account for a couple of days. There were querulous complaints from a couple of old clients and a number of new enquiries, which meant more work but also hopefully prompt payments.

Jo built websites for companies and individuals. She loved her work; it was challenging and creative and satisfying. Working from home was a benefit, too, as it meant she could keep Maureen company. She had to go to meetings with clients of course, but she quite liked driving about to different locations to meet people. Her business was doing well, and it had been very pleasing to make enough profit to take her family on holiday.

Later she put on her sunglasses and a

pair of beaten leather sandals and went down the winding path to the village. She'd worked hard all morning until her head was spinning. It was hard concentrating when the sun was shining and the workmen singing. Frau Hiss had brought her coffee and tray bakes mid-morning. Before Jo was hungry again, she'd been served a wonderful lunch of dark rye bread, slivers of salami and a wedge of strong cheese. A glass cup of peppermint tea was the perfect accompaniment.

She thought of Gav and his café. He'd love to hear about the dishes eaten here. Thinking of him made her think of Maureen, which reminded her that she'd meant to ask Stella if she'd phoned home yet. Jo had messaged her mother about her safe arrival and told her that she'd found Stella. But it was up to her sister to apologise and explain to Maureen what was going on. Needless to say, Stella wasn't up despite it being midday.

Jo was determined not to let her

concerns about her family spoil the day. She stepped firmly onto the pavement in the village square, the cobbled stones hot under her soles. Eager to explore, she wandered around, enjoying the sensation of not being in a hurry. Too much of her life usually was run at pace and at others' beck and call. Here, it was very pleasant to simply look.

The houses were all old, with half-timbers and painted shutters. Most had red roof tiles, and Jo noticed that the tall spire of the church was topped with a gold weather vane. Behind a row of houses was a small cliff of the soft yellow loess soil the region was famous for. Above the roofs were rows of vines on the hilltop.

On the main street she found the *Bäckerei,* the baker's shop, with a window display of wheaten loafs, poppy-sprinkled pretzels and fruit tarts. Beside it was the *Metzgerei,* the butcher's shop, full of more varieties of sausages than Jo had ever seen. The next shop sold dried flower arrangements and gorgeous pottery jugs and bowls. She went inside and was greeted in a friendly fashion by the young woman behind the counter. On discovering Jo was an English tourist, she couldn't help enough.

'We don't get many foreign tourists here. I hope you like our village and the Kaisersuhl? This is great for me to practise my English.'

'I haven't seen much of the area yet, but I'm looking forward to it. I love these jugs.'

'These are local designs. Which do you like? This one?' She held up a jug with clustered grapes and vine leaves and an inscription.

'It's lovely. What does it say?'

'*Trink aus Stein den Edlen Wein*. It means drink out of stoneware the . . . how do you say . . . heavenly wine. Quite a fun rhyme.'

'I'll take it, please,' Jo said impulsively.

The strap of her sandal suddenly

snapped off. Jo made a face. Her sandals were old but she'd hoped they'd last longer. However, the leather had clearly been too stressed to last. She knelt and tried to reattach the strap.

'There's a clothing shop at the top of the street,' the girl said helpfully. 'It's called Muller. You can get new shoes there.'

'Thanks.' Jo paid for the jug, now beautifully wrapped in tissue paper, and with a wave to her new friend went out and turned up the street. She'd just about make it, limping up.

Luckily the shop wasn't far away. It had a pink awning and the word 'Muller' splashed brightly in glittering gold across it. The windows had mannequins wearing summer dresses and culottes, with rainbow cotton scarves wrapped jauntily around their necks. The whole effect was one of holiday freedom. Something sparked in Jo's chest; a yearning for the carefree mood that was being sold here.

She pushed open the door and went into the cool interior, where she slid off her broken sandal and its partner and stuffed them into her bag. Barefoot, she looked about. A teenage girl came out from the back room. She was slim and dark-haired, and her glance took in Jo's feet.

'Hello. I've had a bit of an accident with my sandals. I'd like to buy a new pair,' Jo said.

'Of course. What sort are you looking for?' the girl answered in good English, with just a trace of an accent.

'Anything that'll allow me to walk about.' Jo smiled. 'I don't mind what style, as long as they're sturdy and the straps won't break.'

The girl looked faintly shocked. 'But you must have some idea what you like. We have walking sandals and Roman strap sandals, or there are styles with heels and so on. What colour do you want?'

This was where Jo missed Stella. Jo didn't care about fashion as long as she was comfortable. Stella, on the other hand, knew what was 'in' and what shouldn't be worn with what. Usually Jo didn't care; she'd far too many more serious things to concern her. But now, that faint feeling of summer freedom echoed. A breeze wafting in from an open window in the shop brought in the scents of warm petals and spiced sausages. Here she was, abroad unexpectedly, and who knew when she'd have another opportunity to indulge herself. Besides, she had a sudden childish urge to prove Stella wrong. She'd accused Jo of being too serious and older than she ought to be.

'Perhaps you have a selection of sandals I could try on?' Jo said. 'And I'd like a dress too.'

Now the girl smiled and nodded. She circled the shop interior and brought back items for Jo to consider. Jo slipped on pairs of sandals while the girl advised. She liked a pair of pale green leather sandals with a low heel. It was all very well trying to be stylish, but she had to be able to walk in them too.

'I'd like these, please. Are you running this shop by yourself? You look very young. I'm Jo, by the way.'

'I'm Petra, and I'm helping my mum in the shop at weekends and after school. Once it's the holidays I'll be in here every day. Mum's in the back, so don't worry, I'm not alone.' There was a flash of amusement in her blue eyes.

'Sorry, I didn't mean to be rude about your age. I think it's great you're working.'

'Did you want a dress?' Petra said, going to a rack and bringing back a couple. 'I think this green one would match your new sandals.'

'It's lovely,' Jo agreed. 'I'd like to try it on to check the size, but I do like the embroidery round the neckline and hem.'

Petra looked really pleased. 'I designed and made this myself.'

'I'm very impressed. So you're a dress designer?' Jo said in astonishment.

Petra blushed, and it reminded Jo

how young she was. She guessed the girl to be about fifteen or sixteen.

'I'd like to be a designer, yes, but at the moment I'm in the shop and I sew alterations mostly. I've made just a few dresses to see if they sell.'

Jo knew she'd buy the dress even if it didn't fit. It was admirable that someone so young had so much drive and ambition. If only Stella showed similar determination. She tried the dress on in the cramped changing room behind a curtain and was glad when it fitted. As she came out she heard an exchange in German. A woman she guessed was Petra's mother was out on the shop floor putting the sandals back on the shelves. She was like her daughter, dark-haired and blue-eyed, but with a more rounded figure. Jo guessed she was about the same age as herself, mid-thirties at most.

'The dress fits perfectly,' she said, 'so I'll take it to go with my sandals, thanks.'

Petra moved forward but her mother took the dress. 'I'll take this for you. Would you like it wrapped?'

'Yes, please.' Jo smiled her thanks at Petra as the girl slipped past her and into the back room. She felt a slight annoyance on Petra's behalf. Surely she should have been allowed the satisfaction of ringing up the sale. Her mother was making it quite clear who was in charge.

'So you are staying in the village on holiday?' the woman asked politely, taking Jo's money and exchanging it for a beautifully wrapped parcel.

'Yes, I'm staying up at the Eisen Castle.'

'With Max?' This was said sharply.

Jo looked up from her bag, where she was stowing her purchases. 'Are you a friend of his?' 'You should go now. Goodbye.' The woman vanished into the back of the shop, leaving Jo with her mouth open.

* * *

Tired and thirsty and out of sorts, Jo hauled herself up the never-ending path to Max's home. All she wanted was a long, cold drink and a lie-down in a cool room. Instead she got Stella.

'I'm not going home, whatever you say.' Stella stood in her way, hands on hips, looking furious. 'Mum's been horrible to me down the phone and there's no way I'm living with her sniping in my ear. So you can go back, but I'm staying here with Max.'

'For goodness sake, it's not all about you,' Jo remonstrated with her. 'What about Gav? You can't just leave him in the lurch when you work at his café. What about Max? Does he want you living in his house for weeks on end? And what about Andy? He's possibly the most important person in all this, but you never even mentioned him.'

'Don't get all sarcastic and older-sister with me,' Stella shouted. 'It's my life, not yours. I didn't ask you to come over here to drag me home. Why are you here? Just go!'

Jo tried to calm down. It wasn't easy in the heat, but someone had to be the sensible one. 'Why don't we get a drink and then discuss it?'

'There's nothing to discuss,' Stella said as she stalked away. 'I know what I'm doing. Do you?'

Jo waited until she'd got a drink of water before she approached Stella again. Her sister was lying on one of the loungers on the terrace with a sulky twist to her mouth. 'Let's talk,' she said, keeping her tone mild. 'I'm sure Mum didn't mean to upset you. She's worried about you, and so am I. So is Andy. Even if you're angry with me for coming here, don't Mum and Andy deserve some answers?'

Stella glared at her. 'It's none of your business. Do you know what I think?'

'No, but I'd like to hear it.'

'You won't want to hear it, but I bet I'm right. You didn't come here for me, did you, Jo? You came here to find Max.'

5

'That's ridiculous.' But even as she formed the words, Jo wondered if they were true. After all, she hadn't tried to talk her way out of coming here; she'd gone along with Maureen's urging for her to follow her sister and bring her home. Couldn't she have simply persuaded Stella over the phone to do so? Wasn't there a part of her that had been curious to finally meet Max in person? Of course there was, Jo thought, trying to be honest with herself. She and Max had been friends for so many years without seeing each other that it was only to be expected that she wanted to meet him. But not like this; not with her worries about her sister's lifestyle. No, she decided, seeing Max had not been a factor in her decision to agree to travel to Germany.

'That's ridiculous,' she repeated more

firmly. 'I'm concerned about you, not Max. Do you know what I think?' She used Stella's words deliberately back at her.

Stella frowned. 'What?'

'I think you're trying to deflect me by mentioning Max. Look, I know you're upset. We can talk later.'

'I don't want to talk later, or any time.'

'Some decisions have to be made,' Jo said as gently as possible. 'Like I said, is this fair to Gav, who's employing you? Or to Max, who's housing you?'

Stella sat up and hugged her knees. She looked suddenly very young and uncertain. Jo's heart went out to her. Her sister's emotions were so easy to read. She lived on impulses and hadn't yet learned to curb them.

'Gav won't mind,' Stella said, glancing up with her large blue eyes at Jo. 'You know he won't. Lizzie does all the real work anyway. I'm Gav's project, and it's a long-term one.'

Jo smiled. Her little sister was more

perceptive than she gave her credit for. 'And Max? Do you really think he's okay with us both staying here?'

'I think Max is man enough to tell us the truth. If he minded us being here, he'd find a way to tell us tactfully. Right? Thing is, I have this feeling that in an odd way, Max needs us. He gives off an aura of loneliness. Maybe we're just what he needs.'

Jo raised an eyebrow. Wow. She'd just learned something about her sister she'd never suspected. Stella had developed empathy. Sometimes it felt like all she cared about was herself, but now she was showing a whole new side. Finally, Jo's little sister seemed to be growing up.

'Okay,' she said, 'that's Gav and Max out of the way. What about Andy?'

Stella flushed. 'I don't want to talk about Andy.'

'Well, if you won't talk about Andy, we'll talk about Mum. She only has your best interests at heart.'

'She wants me to come straight

home.' Stella sighed. 'And she gave me a massive telling-off for frightening her.'

'Mum has a dramatic streak, we both know that. But she'll be missing you. You know she's not good on her own.'

'That reminds me — she wants you to ring her back as soon as you get in.'

'What about?' Jo asked, puzzled.

'I don't know. Some man had called her from the bank. She didn't sound too happy with you either.' Stella said this with a certain amount of satisfaction.

Jo's head began to ache. A pain wrapped itself around her temples and beat in time with her heart. She'd no idea who Maureen was talking about. Still, at least Stella's mood had brightened. Her sister was admiring her polished nails and humming a tune under her breath.

She glanced at Jo and smiled. 'Are we good? I don't like it when we argue. It's summer, and it's wonderfully hot, and here we are in Germany in a beautiful castle with Max. Let's not waste it shouting at each other.'

Jo refrained from saying that actually it was Stella who'd been shouting. With years of learned patience behind her, however, she managed a nod. 'You're quite right. Let's be friends.' As her sister turned to go outside, Jo called her name and waited until she'd paused on the step. 'I can't force you to go home, but I want you to think about all the things we've talked about. I hope you'll know when it's time to leave here.'

Stella froze for a moment, one foot hovering over the step. Then she put it down and walked away without answering. Jo sighed. She had to believe that her sister would mull over their conversation until she realised Jo was right. It was all very well enjoying the summer here in Max's fairytale castle, but it wasn't real life for them; it was a bubble. At some point the bubble had to burst and Stella would have to face facts.

Jo waited until she heard the scrape of the sun lounger, and then stepped out of earshot. Finding her mobile in her bag, she rang her mother.

Maureen didn't waste a moment on pleasantries. She sounded upset, and her voice was high and reedy over the connection. 'Why was someone ringing you from the bank? He said . . . he said you've got a mortgage. What does he mean?'

Jo's headache lifted briefly. There was a pulse of excitement. The bank had approved her mortgage. This was swiftly followed by a flicker of fear. It was real — she could get a mortgage, and that meant she could buy her flat. Which meant . . . Her thoughts tumbled one after another like falling masonry. Living on her own . . . being independent or lonely, depending on the viewpoint . . . a whole new stage of life.

Some days, when she felt strong and confident, Jo would mentally shake herself. *For goodness sake, I'm thirty years old. I have my own business, which is doing well, and I really ought to be living in my own apartment by now!* She imagined trotting down a street in expensive high heels, clutching a takeaway coffee just like women in the movies. But there were other days when her confidence was stabbed by negative thoughts. What if her business failed? What if no one needed new websites anymore? Worse, she imagined waking up each day to a silent, empty flat where there was no company. Of course she worked from home, so there'd be no escape from it.

'Jo? Are you still there?'

'Sorry, Mum. Yes, I'm still here. I was going to tell you, but then this thing with Stella came up. I've been looking at flats to buy.'

There was a long silence at the other end of the phone. Jo's headache was back with a vengeance. Then: 'You're moving out of our home?' There was a tremble in her mother's voice which made Jo's heart sink.

What had she been thinking? She knew how vulnerable Maureen was. She'd been caring for her all these years. She and Stella both tried to keep any unpleasant news from their mother. Stress wasn't good for her. Jo had been running their home, doing the family finances, buying the weekly shop and generally keeping them all going. If she moved out, how could she keep doing that? And yet . . . Jo wondered when her own life was going to begin.

'Nothing's certain,' she said now, already soothing her mother. 'I've been researching it, that's all.'

'I don't know how I'd cope if you left home,' Maureen said, and Jo heard a sniffle.

'Please don't worry about it, Mum. It was just a silly idea, that's all. Of course I'm not moving out. I won't leave you.'

'Oh, darling, I'm so glad to hear that. It's bad enough that Stella's not here. What would I do without you? When are you two coming home?'

'I'm not sure. We'll be back before the summer ends, but right now I think maybe Stella needs some breathing space and a chance to think about things.'

Jo realised she was also talking about herself. The blow of giving up the chance of buying her own flat had ramped up her headache to a raging pain. She hadn't been sure it was the right decision, but she had wanted to make that decision by herself. Now that had been torn out of her hands. She couldn't leave Maureen; it was clear her mother wasn't going to cope without her. Jo wished she'd been able to have a conversation about it before her mother found out from the bank. There might've been some way, some compromise to be made. Now it was over.

'I've got to go. I love you.' She pressed the button to end the call.

When taking a couple of painkillers didn't help, Jo found her way out of the castle gardens and up into the vineyards. She blundered along a dusty path between two green rows of ripening grapes, her vision blurred. Furiously, she rubbed her eyes dry. There was no point in crying over something that couldn't be mended.

At the highest point of the vines, she sank down onto the grass and rested her head on her bent knees. Here it was a little cooler. She was surrounded by regimented rows of vines planted in the yellow soil, radiating out and downhill from the spot where she sat; and the shade of a giant horse chestnut filtered over her at the pinnacle.

'Everything all right?'

Jo's head shot up at the sound of Max's voice. He came towards her through the vines, brushing the dark green leaves aside. His grey eyes were concerned.

Jo forced a smile. 'Fine, really. I didn't know you were back.'

He sat carefully beside her, with enough space so that they didn't touch. Yet Jo was very conscious of him, as if the air vibrated between them.

'What is it, Jo? You looked a little defeated when I saw you just now. Tell me what it is.'

'It's nothing . . . ' Then, despite saying that, Jo found herself telling him about the phone call with Maureen and about her hopes of buying her own flat. Max listened without interruption until she finished with a sigh. There was a silence, and Jo suddenly wished she hadn't spoken. After all, she hardly knew him. Why had she offloaded her emotions so easily onto him? *Because he's Max. It's like writing him those letters of long ago.* She glanced up slowly. What was he thinking of her?

'It's not easy, making a decision so serious,' Max said at length. 'I can understand why you want your own place, but I can see why Maureen doesn't want to let you go.'

'So you can't solve it for me?' Jo said with a shaky laugh. It was a weak attempt at a joke.

Max grinned at her. 'Did I ever solve any of your problems? Or you, mine? I don't think so. But maybe just by being there and writing back, we helped each other.'

'That's true,' Jo said. 'This is so big, I need to work it through myself. I was being lazy hoping you'd tell me what to do.'

'I can't imagine you being lazy,' Max said.

'You don't know me well enough to say that.'

'True, I don't know the grown-up Jo, but I knew the girl, and she didn't strike me as lazy. She was always making big plans, and was very determined to study hard and look after her family. I don't think you have changed in that, have you?'

Jo shook her head. Maybe Max had answered for her after all. She couldn't abandon her family even now. Maureen needed her, and Jo had to put that first. She looked back at Max and saw sadness in his face once more. 'I had a weird experience this afternoon,' she said, trying to break his mood and scanning her brain for a topic to discuss.

'What was that?' He seemed to relax

a little, leaning back against the trunk of the old tree.

'I went into the village and found a dress shop. I bought some stuff and was chatting to the owner. But when I mentioned your name she practically threw me out.'

'Ah, so you've met Sylvie then.'

'Who is she?' Jo leaned back, too, and found the solid strength of the tree trunk quite reassuring against her spine.

'Sylvie is my ex-wife.'

She hadn't expected him to say that! Her mental image of the boutique and its inhabitants shifted like angles of light change the colour of a room. 'And Petra . . . Is she your . . . ?' The pieces clicked together in Jo's mind as Frau Hiss's conversation came back to her. Max had a daughter.

'My daughter, yes. Sylvie and I were married very young. It was a mistake, and we both knew it as soon as we started living together as a married couple. So many arguments. We clashed over everything — how to spend our limited money, how to bring up a baby, big important things.'

'I'm sorry.' This was a side of Max she knew nothing about. It was about the adult she'd never got to meet.

He shrugged. 'It's in the past now. Well, that is, my relationship with Sylvie is. With Petra, it's a different matter.'

He stopped for a moment and Jo thought he'd finished. She was curious to know more, but felt guilty for prying into his life. She wouldn't prompt him. If he wanted to tell her, he would.

'When we split up, Sylvie got married again very quickly to Pierre, a Frenchman. Petra was just a baby, and we decided it was better for her if I stayed out of her life. She has a stable family with two parents.'

'But that's awful.' Jo sat up and stared at Max, suddenly more involved than she'd promised herself to be. 'You're Petra's father — surely she has a right to know that.'

He held up a hand to stop her

outburst and threw her a smile. 'It wasn't that bad. Petra knows I'm her father; and for a while, when she was little, she came to spend some time with me each week.'

'And when she was older?'

Max sighed deeply. 'Now I have a problem. Petra is growing up so fast, and I'm scared I'm missing out on really getting to know my daughter. But Sylvie insists it's better that Petra doesn't see me. She says it'll only confuse her. Being a teenager is hard enough without adding complications.'

'What does Petra say?' Jo asked, thinking that Sylvie sounded cold-hearted towards Max.

'I haven't spoken to her directly. I have to respect Sylvie's wishes as her mother. Perhaps she's right. I know Pierre has been a good father to her, and maybe I'm upsetting the apple cart by trying to get to know her better.'

'You don't seriously believe that, do you? It has to be better for her to know her own father.' Jo thought about her own dad and how much she'd loved him. Petra's life had to be enriched by knowing both her step-dad and her own dad, surely?

'I have a friend, Franz, who is a lawyer. He wants me to take legal action against Sylvie and force her to allow me access to my daughter. But I don't believe that will solve my problem. At the moment, I'm waiting and hoping that Sylvie will change her mind.'

'Don't you bump into her in the village? Living in such a small community, how can you avoid it?'

'I'm not in the village very much,' Max said. 'I'm either here working in the vineyard or out of town on business. Frau Hiss orders the food and sorts the household. I've no reason to go there much.'

He flexed his shoulders and stood up, and Jo realised their conversation was over. Poor Max. No wonder he had an aura of sadness. Jo had a sudden desire to help him. She'd no idea how, but somehow she had to get Max and Petra together. Sylvie was wrong; it was completely unfair to keep father and daughter apart.

She stood up, too, and they began to go back down towards the castle. There was a sweet, rich scent of plants in the air, and above them a flock of swifts swooped and dived for insects in the heat.

'Max?' Jo said.

He turned back to her with a raised eyebrow in query.

'Did you mean what you said, about not minding if Stella and I stay for a while?'

'I wouldn't have said it otherwise. Please stay as long as you wish.'

'Just for a while,' she repeated. 'We'll be gone before the summer ends. I'll pay for our food and board. I don't want us to be a burden to you.'

Max laughed, and for once his expression was unguarded and happy. 'There's no need for that. Frau Hiss always buys far too much and bullies me to eat more. I'm delighted for you and Stella to share my burden. You'll be doing me a favour.'

Jo's heart skipped a beat. His teeth flashed white against his tanned skin, and the line of his jaw was strong. A little shiver played down her neck. She cast her glance away, confused. Yes, he was an extremely attractive man. But he showed no interest that way in her. He was friendly, but that was all. Besides, in a few short weeks she'd be gone. What was the point in pursuing her physical reaction to him?

Who was she kidding, anyway? She was plain old Jo, and she had commitments of a different kind. Maureen needed her, and so did Stella, even if she didn't know it. Max was hardly likely to fall smitten at her feet. That was a good thing, wasn't it?

6

The weeks flew by. Sometimes it seemed to Max as if Jo and Stella had always been there, a part of his family keeping him company. He'd begun to enjoy the fact that there were other people around him. Stella's chattiness still made him want to dive for cover at times, especially if he was tired from a day's work and wished to read. Then he'd make his excuses and escape by shutting the door to his study. But he had to admit that Jo's peaceful presence was something he'd come to depend upon. She was often working too, her dark head bent over her laptop during the day or making calls to clients on her mobile.

In the evenings they often sat together on the terrace, drinking a glass of good German wine and talking about their day. The summer evenings were warm and pleasant, and Max found himself looking forward to those hours when dinner was finished and he could put his worries aside for a while. He hoped that Jo enjoyed those times too. He liked seeing her almond-brown eyes brighten with laughter at some of his stories about his vineyard. He liked the way her glossy brown hair glinted in the candlelight. He liked Jo. Perhaps a little too much.

He was conscious that his guests were only there for the summer, and so he told himself not to get too fond of her — which was hard when she was so easy to talk to and he told her things he usually kept inside his head. It was just like when they were kids, pouring out words onto paper to send to each other. Except they weren't kids. Jo was very much a woman.

'Is it ready?' Stella burst in, breathless as he looked up from his computer.

'You mean the café?'

'Yes, of course I mean the café, Max. I don't hear the builders this morning, and Uwe pretty much told me they'd finished.'

'It's finished.' Max grinned, amused at Stella's enthusiasm. 'Do you want to see it?'

'Oh, yes, I do. Let me get Jo; she'll want to join us.'

Soon they were all standing outside the double glass doors to Max's new café. The café frontage had been carefully built to meld with the old stones of the castle wall. New stones had been chosen in the same honey colour and consistency to fit around the doors.

'Well, aren't you going to open it?' Stella cried impatiently.

For an instant, Max was reluctant to do so. Firstly, the facade was so perfect he wanted to savour the moment. Here was all his hard work now paying off. Secondly, it was as if by opening the door it made his project real. It would either be successful or it would fail, and it all started right now. He looked at Jo and caught her smile. He had the feeling she knew what he was thinking.

Then he reached out and opened the doors. A smell of fresh paint hit his nostrils. Inside, the large room was starkly white. There was no furniture and no curtains or blinds.

'It's lovely,' Jo said beside him.

'The structure is ready,' he said, 'but it's only a shell.'

'Yes,' Stella said, 'you need some blond wood tables and chairs to go with the white paintwork. And what about red and white checked curtains and tablecloths?'

'Stella,' Jo warned, 'it's Max's café. I'm sure he's got his own ideas of what to do.'

'Actually,' Max said, 'I'm happy to get suggestions. I'd only got this far with it. I wanted a good well-built room, but I'm not great with interior design.'

Stella flashed a triumphant smile at Jo. 'You see, we can help Max get set up. It'll be just like when we helped at Mum and Dad's.'

'Do you want to see the kitchen?' Max asked, leading the way.

The café kitchen was small and compact, but there was plenty of storage space, and gaps to allow a cooker and dishwasher to be installed.

'There's still work to be done,' Jo remarked, looking at the empty spaces.

'Yes, it's not ready yet. For a start I need to get a counter for the till and — '

'And to display the cakes,' Stella interrupted. 'You know, so that your customers can browse the selection. Oh, you should go organic; that's so popular now. Imagine all the lovely healthy but delicious bakes you could offer.'

Max was caught up by her infectious enthusiasm. To be honest, he hadn't got further in his thoughts than getting the café built. But now Stella's suggestions made him realise there was a lot more work to be done.

Jo touched his hand, and a spark of pure electricity shot through him. He stepped back, sure she must have felt it too. But when he was able to meet her gaze she seemed as calm as usual. Was it fair that only his heart should be pumping so hard?

'You'll tell us if we're interfering?' she asked with a concerned frown.

'I'm delighted to get your input,' he assured her. 'I think what we need is a planning session. There's all sorts of things I haven't decided on. You both have experience of running a café, so I'm glad of your help.'

'I wouldn't say we have that much experience,' Jo said. 'Stella works part-time as a waitress, and I only have memories of our parents' place. I'm not sure I'll be any good to you.'

Stella broke in, 'You can do Max's publicity. He'll need a website, won't he? Besides, there has to be a grand opening, something a bit special to promote the place.'

'That's a great idea,' Max said. 'You see, I do need you both. I was planning on simply opening it when it's ready, but I like the idea of some kind of event.'

* * *

Uwe was coming to pick Stella up on his motorbike. She smoothed down her dress and checked her hair, then slid her over-large sunglasses down so that no one could read her expression. She was excited by Max's café plans and also by the prospect of driving around the villages on a motorbike. The summer was full of possibilities and new experiences and she wanted to soak them all up, wrap herself in them and feel it all intensely. So it was irritating that a small part of her mind kept flicking back to Andy and the conversation they'd ended up having.

Jo's nagging had forced her to finally pick up the phone to him. She knew she'd get no peace from her sister until she did. It was hard to hear his voice at the other end of the line and to speak. His eager tone on hearing it was her made her feel guilty. That, in turn, made her annoyed. It was as if he was controlling her from far away. It made her want to scream and run all over again.

'Are you coming back?' he'd asked.

Stella stifled a sigh. 'Not yet.' She opened then shut her mouth. There was so much to say and yet so little. She hadn't changed her mind about getting married. And where to start on all the wonderful things about Max's castle and the Kaiserstuhl?

'I love you.'

She sidestepped that. 'I'm sorry I ran off like that. But I need to think about . . . us.'

'It's okay, I understand. Look, we don't have to get married. Can you come home so we can discuss it?'

'Andy, I have to have space. It's the way I am. I can't tell you when I'm coming back or what I'll decide. I can't!' She cut the call and shoved her phone deep into the bottom of her bag, where it rang for a while. After it stopped, she checked the incoming numbers. Of course it was all Andy. Stella bit her lip and stared at the screen. Then she put the phone back in her bag and tried to forget about it.

There was a throaty roar and Uwe appeared, scattering up stones from the drive as he slewed the motorbike round. It was all shiny metal and gleaming red, and quite a bit larger than Stella had imagined it'd be. She was rather nervous, but decided a cool approach suited her look best. After all, she'd spent a good hour getting ready. She pushed her glasses up the bridge of her nose, pushed her hair back, and smiled prettily.

'You look fantastic.' Uwe grinned, getting off the bike with a swagger. 'Ready to see the sights of the region?'

'Of course. I'm looking forward to it. Do I have to wear a helmet?' It was going to mess up her hair, Stella thought in dismay.

Uwe shook his head. 'No need. We're staying on the small roads through the vines. Jump up behind me.'

There was a certain thrill in climbing onto the machine and putting her arms around his waist for balance. *Andy wouldn't like me doing this.* It was really annoying the way he popped into her brain when she least expected it. Determined to ignore Andy and what he might or might not like, Stella gave a laugh with false bravado. 'Let's see how fast it goes, then.'

'Don't worry, it's very fast,' Uwe shouted back proudly and he kicked at the motorbike so the engine revved up noisily. As Stella wondered what she'd got herself into, with a whoosh of grit and fumes Uwe drove off, barely missing Max's wall.

Jo couldn't believe it. She watched out of her bedroom window as Stella and Uwe zoomed off. Not only was Stella not wearing a helmet, but she had her arms around him. Jo wasn't sure which was worse. Visions of her baby sister crashing made her groan. How could Stella be so stupid? And what was going on between her and the young man that Max employed? Was it simply a summer friendship, or was it more? Whatever it was, it wasn't fair on Andy, Jo decided. Then she rubbed her face tiredly. She couldn't bear another argument with Stella.

She shut her laptop with a snap. She hadn't been concentrating on it anyway. Mostly she'd been gazing out the window at the beautiful view and feeling the warm sunshine on her skin. There was something magical about this place. It felt timeless, as if the summer might go on forever. She liked that idea. More than liked it.

When she was able to forget about Maureen and Stella, she enjoyed imagining helping Max open up his café. There had been a definite thrill when she'd touched his hand; a zap that ran from her fingertips right along the nerves of her hand and arm to her heart. Had he noticed too? She didn't think so. After all, she'd meant it as a friendly gesture, nothing more. It wasn't his fault that she was attracted to him more and more each day. Not just his good looks; it was his personality as well. She was getting to know him, and everything she discovered she liked.

She'd come to rely on their evening discussions. It was satisfying to have someone to talk to about her day and how she had to deal with her overbearing or grumpy or demanding clients. Max in turn would explain the running of the vineyards and his hopes for the café and tourism in the castle. Then they would cast more widely for their topics, and gave their opinions on the world in general. Jo was fascinated to hear what Max thought about everything, and was touched that he was such a good listener. At home, no one listened. Stella couldn't sit still long enough, and anyway had no interest in politics or the environment. Maureen wanted Jo to listen to her problems, and it never felt right to burden her mother with her own.

Where was Max now? Jo went

downstairs. It was an excuse to finish up work for a break. She found him in the new café talking to a workman. A solid double oven had been installed along with a large dishwasher in the café kitchen. Max waved to her, then signed a sheet and thanked the man for installing the machines.

'What do you think?' he said.

'They look great. The new counter, too. I can quite imagine it filled with home baking.' They walked back through to the café room to admire it.

'The café still looks bare,' Max remarked. 'There's work to be done before I can open it up.'

'You're nearly there. When are the tables and chairs arriving?'

'Tomorrow. I've ordered crockery, kitchen items and cutlery to arrive then, too. Then all I need is staff to run things. I'll be able to employ people from the village.'

'Don't forget curtains and table-cloths, napkins and so on. There's a lot to remember.'

'I must put those on my ever-expanding list.' Max grinned.

'I hope you get enough customers. The castle isn't on the usual tourist route, is it?'

'Not for foreign tourists, no. But I usually get a good number of German tourists coming through in the summer months for day trips. I don't expect to open the café all year round.'

'If I design you a website, it should bring more people in. That is, if you still want me to?'

'Have you got room for another client? You are so busy, always the head over the laptop.'

Jo smiled back at him. 'To be honest, it'll make a lovely change working with someone who isn't going to shout at me when there are glitches.'

'How do you know I don't shout?' Max teased.

Jo forgot to take a breath. There was a warmth in his expression that made her glow. Or was she imagining it? Because the next minute, he'd turned away and was examining the new electrical sockets.

'I'm going to make a coffee. Can I fix you one?' she asked, searching for a distraction. Without waiting for his answer, she sped out of the café and back into the castle kitchen. The action of heating the water and measuring out the roast grounds relaxed her. She sang to herself, an old English folk song coming into her head, one she'd forgotten about but which at one time had been a favourite.

'Are you still in the choir?'

Max's voice startled her. She dropped a spoon, and the dark grains of coffee scattered onto the counter. She mopped them up, conscious of him nearby. How odd that he remembered her choir. It had all been so long ago.

'I'm not in the choir and I don't really sing these days. Not for an audience, at any rate,' she said, adding the coffee to the pot and smelling its rich scent.

'What a pity. I think you had a

passion for it. What's that song you were singing there?'

''Scarborough Fair'. Do you know it?'

'Wait.' Max disappeared, leaving Jo holding two coffee cups to an empty space. He was soon back, and Jo understood when she saw what he was holding.

'Your mandolin,' she said. 'You wrote me when you got it as a birthday present. Did you learn to play it then? Your letters were full of frustration for a while with the lessons.'

In answer, Max sat and angled the instrument toward himself. His long, mobile fingers found the chords and he strummed the strings until Jo heard the melody of the folk song on the air. The sound of the mandolin was so beautiful it brought up the tiny hairs on the back of her neck.

'Sing with me,' Max coaxed. 'Sing with me, Jo.'

* * *

Stella was hot and dirty and out of sorts. The motorbike stood propped up on its stand with a fine coating of loess soil. Uwe was swilling down a beer as if they'd traversed a desert instead of coasting through the vineyard paths. She was thirsty too, but he hadn't offered to buy her a drink. She rummaged in her bag and found some euros.

They were at a small café somewhere in a tiny village. It smelt of sausages and dust, and her stomach lurched. She'd had no idea it was possible to get travel sick on the back of a motorbike. Uwe went far too fast. Not that she was going to say that. No, it was important to maintain her composure. Slightly shakily, she walked into the café to get a Coke. If they had such a thing. She hoped Max's café would be more modern than this one.

There was a mirror with a crack down its middle on the wall. Stella let out a tiny scream. She looked awful. Why hadn't Uwe said so? Her hair was like a bird's nest and there were streaks of dust on her cheeks. She knew her armpits were horribly damp, and a trickle of sweat was busy running down her spine.

There had been a near miss with a tractor too. They'd gone round a corner at speed and . . . well, Stella didn't want to relive it. Maybe she'd made a mistake coming out today. Not only that, but Uwe kept trying to kiss her, even when she told him she just wanted to be friends. She kind of dreaded going back. She didn't want to sit on that monster bike again, didn't want to die in a freak accident, and most of all she didn't want Uwe getting the wrong idea when she put her arms round him riding pillion.

* * *

Later, Jo went for a walk in the village. Stella wasn't back yet and she wanted to take her mind off that. Max had excused himself to his study to work.

Singing in his presence, in anyone's presence, was a step into the blue for her. She'd given up the choir when her dad died and hadn't sung in company since then. But Max had looked so hopeful, sitting there with his mandolin, that she hadn't had the heart to refuse him. Now she wasn't sure what she felt. So a walk, putting one foot in front of the other, suited her just fine. She didn't have to engage her brain.

Until she came to Sylvie's boutique. It was shut like all the other shops, as it was now evening. She paused and then had a brilliant idea.

7

Well it had seemed like an ideal solution at the time, but now Jo wasn't so sure. Petra looked ill at ease as she stood in the café. It was a few days later, and the tables and chairs had arrived in the meantime. They were sturdy blond-wood furniture, just as Stella had suggested, and Jo thought they looked just right in the white-painted brightly lit room.

'Is my father home today?' Petra asked, digging her hands into her skirt pockets.

'No, he's got business in the city,' Jo said.

Which was why she'd chosen today to ask Petra to meet her here. Max needed curtains and tablecloths for the café, and Petra was a budding seamstress. It was a perfect match. At least, Jo had thought so as she had stood outside Sylvie's closed boutique. Now Petra's obvious nerves were affecting her too. What would Max think once he found out? Had Jo really done the right thing? And what about Sylvie's reaction when she discovered Jo had manipulated a connection between father and daughter without consulting her?

Petra stared at the empty counter and the six tables with their neat ring of chairs. The café had an air of anticipation. All it needed was food and customers for its life to begin, Jo thought. She watched the slim girl as she stood there. She should have realised this was Max's daughter the day she met her. Although she had her mother's dark hair and blue eyes, the way she held herself and her mannerisms were so like Max.

'Maybe this was a mistake,' Petra said, leaning down to grab her cloth bag at her feet.

'No, wait! Please wait,' Jo said quickly.

'I don't think my mother will approve

of me being here.' Petra slung the bag across her shoulder.

'It's just . . . it's just that the café needs some fabric, curtains and tablecloths, and I thought of you. You're a seamstress and I don't know of any other, being a foreigner here. I'm trying to help Max.'

'But you know that I'm not meant to see him, right?' Petra said shrewdly.

Jo sighed and sat down on the nearest chair. 'Look, you're right. Probably this was a bad idea. But can we at least have a chat about it? Won't you take a seat for a moment?'

Petra hesitated, the chunky bag oversized on her slim frame. Then she dropped the bag with a soft thud. She slid gracefully into the chair opposite Jo, put her chin on her palms and waited. The gesture was obvious, Jo thought with an internal grin. Jo had asked Petra here, so it was up to Jo to explain and take responsibility for it. Very well, she'd give it a go!

'Max misses you and he wants to get

to know you. Surely you want to see him?'

'It's not that simple,' Petra said quietly. 'My mother isn't happy with me seeing him.'

'What about you? What do you want?'

'I want to keep everybody happy.'

'Even if that means missing out on a relationship with your dad?' Jo couldn't imagine how she'd bear the situation Petra found herself in. She'd loved her own dad so very much. He'd understood her. She loved Maureen too, of course she did, but it had always been a much more difficult relationship. Her mother needed her; leaned on her. Jo tried to think back to the happy days when both her parents were alive and busy with the restaurant. In those days Jo was daddy's girl, while Stella was doted upon by their mother. Not much had changed in that way. Stella was still the apple of Maureen's eye and could do no wrong. But Jo had lost out. Her father's death had left a painful gap in her life that could not be filled. How would she have felt to grow up never having really known him? It was unimaginable.

'It's very difficult,' Petra said. 'I don't want to upset my mum. She thinks if I spend time with my father then somehow it'll mess me up. Pierre doesn't mind me making contact, so I don't understand why she does. But if I mention it, she gets mad.'

'Wouldn't this be a way to persuade her otherwise? You'd be doing a proper job here, gaining experience.' It sounded feeble, even to Jo. Petra was right, this was a mistake.

'I want to do it,' Petra said. 'It would be great to run off some samples for my father to choose from. Tablecloths are so easy and quick to make. The curtains take longer, but I can make them. I've made up some for home.'

There was an enthusiasm in her voice when she spoke about sewing. It was clear to Jo that it was a vocation for the girl. How could they make this situation work? 'Would it help if I talked to Sylvie?' she offered.

'I don't think it will make any difference, to be honest. Her mind is made up.'

'Then I was wrong to ask you here. I'm sorry I've wasted your morning. Look, I'll walk with you back to the village. I've got some shopping to pick up.'

'Please don't apologise,' Petra said. 'I'm glad to have a look at the castle. I wish . . . I wish things could be different.'

'Let me just go and get my purse and we can go.'

* * *

For once, Stella was happy to have peace and quiet. Frau Hiss had gone home, and she had permission from the older woman to use the castle kitchen as long as she left it tidy. That was a challenge, as usually when she cooked at home she left a tsunami of dirty pans and utensils which Maureen cleared up for her. However, she'd turned over a new leaf, she decided. She was going to do some baking, try out some recipes for Max's café, and leave the place spotless.

She saw Jo and a girl leaving and wondered who she was. Maybe it was one of Max's employees from the vineyard. She flicked through some recipes on her phone and forgot about the girl. Yes, there were some really lovely desserts, tray bakes and meringues she could make.

Humming a little tune, Stella pulled out baking trays, mixing bowls and a set of scales that Frau Hiss had pointed out. As she measured out sugar, flour and butter she found herself absorbed in her task. She wasn't thinking about Andy or Maureen or Jo. The sweet aromas swirled around her as she worked. She was going to be a good cook. She had made cakes at home and they were okay. Mostly. Sometimes she made the evening meal, when she felt like it. Besides, it made her feel . . . *contented*. That was the word. Stella nodded with satisfaction.

If only Dad hadn't died and Mum hadn't let the family restaurant go. Those were the only truly happy memories she had. Growing up, she'd often felt guilty in some undefined way when Maureen was crying or took to her bed unwell. Jo had been more of a mother to her, but she'd missed her own mum.

She glanced out the window and saw a thin cat jump onto the wall. Quickly she placed the biscuits she'd made onto a baking tray and slid them into the oven. Now the cat was meowing.

'Are you hungry? You look like a stray.'

She filled a saucer with milk and took it outside. The cat came down from the wall, its tail straight up with the tip curved over in a question mark. Stella hunkered down and stroked its soft fur while it drank. A raggedy purr filled the air.

'And who are you? I can't quite imagine Max owning a cat. He looks more like a dog person to me.'

She sat down beside her new companion and basked in the sunshine. The cat's fur was delightfully warm under her fingertips. A sleepiness stole over her. Her eyelids fluttered shut just for a moment.

A shrieking alarm split the silence. The cat shot up over the wall and disappeared. Stella leapt up too. What on earth . . . ? Then she remembered the biscuits. With a wail, she ran into the kitchen. Smoke was puffing out from the oven door. She turned the heat off and grabbed an oven glove, opened the door and coughed. Waving away the smoke, she pulled the baking tray out with dismay. It was dotted with small blackened lumps. *Her biscuits.*

Stella put the tray into the sink and poured cold water over it until the burning and smoking had stopped. She stared at it. She was truly useless. Jo was right. Oh, she didn't come directly out and say so, but it was obvious she was a disappointment. She had failed at everything. Being a daughter. Being a waitress. Being a girlfriend. Stella sank down onto the cool flagged tiles and let the tears come.

* * *

The look on Max's face said everything. He knew. His grey eyes were cold. Jo swallowed. She was back in the castle and it was now late afternoon. She'd walked with Petra into the village and waved goodbye at the top of the winding road where she lived. Then she'd wandered aimlessly, picked up her shopping, done some window shopping and enjoyed the summer heat. Returning to the terrace, she'd looked for Stella, but there was no sign of her. A pile of trays and dishes formed a small mountain on the draining board in the kitchen, and there was a lingering smell of something burnt. Apart from that, the place was silent.

She gripped her laptop now as Max stalked over to her. Whatever he was going to say, she deserved it.

'How could you, Jo,' he said quietly. Somehow his steely coldness was worse than if he were shouting. 'I came back through the village, only to have my car flagged down by an irate Sylvie. She says Petra was here and that you invited her.'

Jo wanted to hide behind the laptop lid. Instead, she took a deep breath. 'I'm sorry; it was a mistake. I thought — '

'You thought wrong! This is between my family and me. It's nothing to do with you.'

Jo flushed. He was absolutely right. She had stuck her nose in where it wasn't wanted, and now she had to pay the price. If only she could explain to him why she'd done it. 'I just wanted — ' But Max shook his head and she fell silent.

'You don't realise what damage you've done. I wanted Sylvie to trust me. I was going to take it slowly and hopefully persuade her to give me joint custody without a legal battle. But now . . . ' He shrugged his powerful shoulders.

'You could wait forever,' Jo cried, 'but if Sylvie saw how happy Petra was here, doing the sewing for the café, surely she'd come round to it being a regular thing.'

Max made a noise as if he despised her. Then he spun on his heel and walked away fast. Jo sat stock still. What had she done? What had she been thinking? At home, it was always her job to come up with solutions to any family problem. But she wasn't at home now. She was in Max's domain. And she didn't know him that well. No matter that she felt she did.

She hadn't helped at all. She'd only made things worse.

* * *

Max went into his study and shut the door firmly. He took a deep breath and stood for a minute. Then he thumped his fists down hard on the desk. The pain was sudden, and cleared his mind like a sluice of iced water. He'd made a mistake. He should never have told Jo and Stella they could stay. He had had peace before they arrived. The castle was always silent. Frau Hiss knew to do her work and then disappear. By the time he finished his work in the vineyards, he had the place to himself. Then he'd take his dinner upstairs and do his accounts with no interruptions.

He had to tell them to go. Tomorrow. Yes, tomorrow he'd say that. He could hardly throw them out this evening. He felt a sudden rush of guilt as he remembered Jo's distressed face. But she deserved his anger. She didn't have the right to interfere in his life, Max argued to himself, pacing the room and unable to settle. It didn't matter if she thought she was doing the right thing. It was nothing to do with her!

So why did he feel a pang of loneliness even now at the thought of her leaving? He was being ridiculous. Once they had gone, all would be back to normal, just the way he liked it. He sat in his leather armchair, fingers steepled under his chin, and stared at the cream-coloured wall. His mind was a blank. How long he remained like that he wasn't sure, until he was interrupted by a firm knock at the door.

Certain that it was Jo, Max hesitated. He didn't know how to react to her. After all, he'd pretty much frozen her out with his anger. Where did they go from here? He didn't know. He was still inclined to tell her and Stella that they had to go.

He opened the door, but it wasn't Jo. Instead, Sylvie stood there. Max stepped back in shock. 'What are you doing here?' he said, wrong-footed. His ex-wife hadn't visited him at the castle for years, not since Petra was tiny, when he was allowed a few precious hours with her. Normally he and Sylvie communicated by phone or messaging, and only when absolutely necessary.

She sighed. 'Can I come in?'

'Yes, yes of course. Here, take a seat. Is there something wrong? Is Petra — '

'Nothing's wrong, Petra's fine. Well, I mean there's no emergency. But actually, I *am* here to talk about Petra.'

'Look, I'm sorry about earlier. I had no idea Petra was here. It was a mistake, but my friend meant everything for the best.' He wasn't going to blame Jo in front of Sylvie.

'Your friend? Who is she?' Sylvie's eyes were bright with sharp curiosity.

'A girl I once knew.' He was reluctant to explain further, not to Sylvie. Not until he knew her motive for coming here today, and what her angle was. Sylvie never did anything on impulse. So what did she want now?

'She came to the boutique. She seems nice, but I was surprised to hear she was staying here. Not with Max, I thought. Max guards his privacy. But it seems she's not alone either. There's another young woman staying here. What is going on?'

Her voice was bright and teasing, but Max didn't react. Sylvie was a great one for worming secrets out of people. Knowledge was power, after all.

'Nothing is going on, as you put it. I've a couple of friends staying here on holiday. What did you want?'

She shrugged as if to say, *Well, I tried.* 'Me? Well, I don't want anything for myself. It's Petra I'm here to talk about.'

'So you said.' Max waited her out.

Sylvie stood up and traced a finger across the bookcase, then walked to stand at the window sill. She stood outlined in the light. 'Petra wants to work here,' Sylvie said eventually.

Max quelled a brief excitement. 'You'd let her?'

'I don't want her to, but she's been very . . . determined.'

'She's not a child anymore,' Max said gently. 'She's a young woman who knows her own mind.'

'She thinks she knows what she wants. What it is to be fifteen and know better than your mother.' Sylvie gave a bitter laugh.

'What's the problem, really? Petra loves you and Pierre. Isn't there room for her to get to know her father too? Are you afraid she'll want to come and live here instead?'

There was a flicker of fear in Sylvie's gaze and Max realised he'd hit the problem head on. Sylvie wasn't as tough as she liked to make out.

'How about this,' he said. 'Petra comes to help out with the café furnishings, but I make it very clear that moving in here is not an option. I'm not looking to break up your family, Sylvie. That has never been my intention. Pierre is a good man and has been a very good step-father. And you're a wonderful mother. But I'd like to be more of a father to Petra, it's true. Can't we give this a go?'

'I can't stop it. I'll tell you the truth — I don't like it, and I don't want her to come here, but I don't believe I can prevent it. She's so set upon this action.

So . . . let it happen.'

'I'd rather it happened with your blessing.'

She shook her head. 'I can't give that. Petra's going to get mixed up. Teenage years are difficult enough without adding to it.'

'What does Pierre say?' Max asked, knowing the Frenchman was sensible and had a relaxed attitude to life.

'He says we have to respect our daughter's views.'

Max tried not to mind that Sylvie, even now, was making it clear that he wasn't to be a part of Petra's family. But she was his daughter too, and even if Sylvie didn't like that, she couldn't change it.

'Pierre's right,' he said. 'So let's set a time for Petra to come and see me.'

After Sylvie had left, Max did a victory dance in his study. Then he slid to a halt. There was one more thing he had to do that evening. He had to apologise to Jo.

8

Jo kept working. Her fingers flew across her keyboard and she filled her mind with facts and figures; anything to keep the thought of Max at bay. It was clear she and Stella couldn't stay on after the argument. Perhaps it was for the best, she mused. Her fingertips stilled on the plastic keys. This way, Stella would be forced to confront her problems. As for Jo . . . well, she'd promised Maureen to stay at home. There wasn't much to look forward to in England. However, she'd plenty of work, and that had to be enough to occupy her.

A shadow crossed her and she glanced up. It was Max. She opened her mouth to say sorry again, but he beat her to it.

'I want to apologise for my behaviour earlier,' he said. 'I was completely out of order.'

'You had every right to be angry. I made a terrible mistake inviting Petra here. It was none of my business.'

'You meant well. You're used to looking after everyone, so I guess that's what you were trying to do here.'

'In a very clumsy manner, yes.' She risked a small smile.

He looked at his watch. 'It's dinner-time. Have you been to Freiburg yet?'

The change of subject threw her. She shook her head.

Max clapped his hands. 'Great. I'm taking you out to dinner in the big city. Ten minutes?'

'But — '

'No more arguments between us, hey? This is my way of making it up to you. So go, get ready.'

She'd never seen him so animated. There was a sparkle in his grey eyes that she hadn't seen before. Something had changed, but what?

Ten minutes wasn't enough. It was a good half hour later before Jo went downstairs to find Max waiting in the hallway. She'd showered and washed her hair, then spread out her clothes on the bed to choose from. She wanted to look pretty but not overdressed; after all, she'd no idea where Max was taking her to dine. In the end she'd gone for the green dress that Petra had made, and slipped on the matching sandals. It was casual and smart and surely fitted most situations.

She paused outside Stella's room. Was the invitation to dinner only for her, or was Stella invited too? The thought of dining alone with Max sent a shiver along Jo's spine. On pushing open Stella's door, she found a slip of paper on the floor. Stella had gone out with Uwe and his friends for a barbecue. Jo wasn't to worry, as she'd be home before midnight.

Jo smiled. At least Stella had been thoughtful enough to leave a note — and one that Jo could find! She hoped her sister had fun with her new German friends and that Uwe behaved himself. She really ought to ask Stella what was going on between them, even if that risked yet another disagreement.

'You look lovely,' Max said softly as she joined him.

'Thank you. You look very smart too,' Jo said, slightly flustered.

Max drove confidently out of the village and onto the motorway. The sky was darkening and a few stars twinkled. The car smelt of leather and pine and a trace of spicy aftershave. Max was wearing a crisp blue and white striped shirt and grey trousers. Jo's nerves tingled as she tried not to stare at him.

She was sitting in an expensive car with a very attractive man, zooming into a foreign city for a lovely dinner. What a change it was from her usual dull life. That tingling of her nerves heightened. She could get used to this. If only Stella could see her now.

'In fact,' Max broke into her thoughts, as if they were continuing their earlier conversation without a break, 'I owe you more than an apology. I owe you a big thank-you.'

'Why?'

'Sylvie came to see me, and she's agreed that Petra can come to the castle and make up the café furnishings.'

'Oh Max, that's wonderful news. I'm so happy for you.'

His hand shot out briefly to cover hers before he returned it to the gearstick. Jo's nerves shot out of control. She couldn't speak. She sneaked a peek at Max out of the corner of her eye and saw that he was grinning like an idiot. What a fool she was; he meant nothing by his gesture. He was quite simply full of happiness about his daughter. Jo's nerves flattened down. She turned to look out the window, but it was dark now, and all she saw was the pale reflection of her face with glittering eyes.

'So we're celebrating,' Max said. 'Petra's coming to visit tomorrow. I'd like you to be there, and Stella. We can finally have our planning meeting about the café.'

'Sounds good.' Jo swallowed a lump

in her throat and tried to sound normal. She must have achieved it, because Max didn't comment.

'So Sylvie's okay with it all?' Jo asked, thinking it was quite a turnaround for Max's ex-wife to make.

'Not entirely. She'd rather Petra didn't get too involved with me, I think, but Petra's got her mind made up.'

'She strikes me as a very determined young lady,' Jo agreed, and they both smiled. *I'm being selfish,* Jo realised. *This moment isn't about me and my growing feelings for Max. It's about Max and Petra. It's wonderful that finally they can meet, even if Sylvie doesn't approve. It's progress. Besides, their family life will go on after I've left.* She tried not to feel sad. This glimpse into the summer delights of Germany and Max's castle — and, yes, Max himself — couldn't continue. Soon she'd be back in the grey skies of home.

'Penny for them?' Max teased.

'Mmm?'

'You were frowning. We can't have

that. I'm taking you to a very special place. Tonight, let's just enjoy ourselves.'

He was right. *Let the future wait,* Jo thought. Max parked the car and they walked out across the cobbled pavements of the beautiful city. Little channels ran alongside, trickling with water. Jo didn't see them immediately and her toe dipped right into the water. Max caught her elbow and steadied her. For a moment, their faces were close. She felt his warm breath caress her skin.

'Be careful of the *bächle,* the little canals. There's an old superstition here that if you fall in you will marry a Freiburg resident.'

'You've had a lucky escape then,' she laughed nervously.

'I was born in Freiburg, don't you remember?'

His hand was still supporting her elbow. The warmth from his grip surged through her. He let her go.

'Come on,' Max said with a nod in

the direction ahead. 'The restaurant is in the main square. I've booked us a table.'

Jo kept up with his long stride, managing to avoid stepping in any more water channels. In amongst the cobbles were pretty mosaics of different patterns. She was going to ask Max why they were there, when they came out into the wide square and she gasped. It was gorgeous. The street lights and the glow from the restaurants and shops around the square showed the beautiful architecture in the buildings. The cathedral was at one corner of the square, its gothic tower proudly touching the sky. Yet more cobblestones and pebble mosaics covered the ground. The air was full of the aromas of cooked food and sweet herbs.

'It's lovely,' Jo exclaimed.

'It's a fine place to spend an evening,' Max agreed, pointing to the open doors of one of the restaurants. 'Let's find our table.'

They were shown to a table for two at

the window and near to the open door. The evening was pleasantly warm, and Jo was glad of her short-sleeved dress. A waiter lit the candle between them and gave them menus. Jo had a view of the square and the intricately carved archway above the entrance to the cathedral. 'I'd like to come back here during the day and visit the church,' she said.

'It is a fine old building,' Max said. 'You should climb the tower; there's great views over the city. Also, there's a market every morning where you can buy fruit and veg, herbs and spices, wood crafts and many more things you didn't know you needed.' There was a gleam of amusement as he watched her.

'You're teasing me, but I don't mind — I'll be coming back to buy all sorts of unsuitable trinkets, you can be sure of that. If you're not careful, I'll bring you back some oddity.'

'I look forward to it.'

Their gazes met. Jo was first to look away. She picked up the menu and pretended to read it. Her heart was beating fast. *This isn't a date*, she told herself. Max was simply being nice, bringing her here. He was happy about Petra and he wanted to share his happiness. It was nothing more.

'So,' Max said, 'what shall we eat?'

'I'll take your advice, as it's all in German,' Jo said, realising she'd been staring at it and not understanding a word.

Max laughed. 'I can get you an English version, if you want.'

'Actually, no. I'll have whatever you're having. Is it German cuisine?'

'Traditional German meals. I thought you might like that. A taste of the Black Forest.'

'Perfect.' It felt very nice indeed to relax and watch the people walking around the old square while Max spoke in rapid German to the waiter.

The food when it came was delicious. They ate spicy and aromatic hunter's stew, which came with wheaten baked bread and sauerkraut. Jo savoured the flavours and the atmosphere. The restaurant was busy but not crowded, and there was a low background murmur as the diners chatted. The waiter brought a bottle of red wine and Max poured two glasses. They glinted in the candlelight, and Jo breathed in deeply as if she could capture the moment forever.

'What are the mosaics all about?' she asked.

'They're medieval advertisements.'

'You're kidding.'

'No, I'm not. If you look at them you'll see scissors or bread baskets showing what kind of shop it was. Nowadays they are decorative only. Nice idea though, isn't it?'

'Ye olde billboards then.' Jo smiled.

'You haven't seen all of them. We can look for more on the way back.'

'But let's not hurry,' she said. 'I don't want this evening to end.'

'I agree! I'm enjoying myself. Summer is racing on too fast.'

'Stella and I have been here several

weeks already. I can hardly believe it. We'll have to go home at some point.'

'Not before the café opens.'

'I wouldn't want to miss that. I'm so glad Petra'll be able to help you get it ready. Do you think Sylvie will let her see you after she's made up the tablecloths?'

'I'm hoping and praying that she sees how content my daughter is with me. So I have to make that happen.'

There was a brief silence between them. Jo filled up the wine glasses, and Max smiled and raised his glass to her. She could hardly look away. She touched his glass with hers. 'Cheers.'

'*Prost.* That's German for cheers. You should learn some of the language,' he teased.

'I'm not very good at languages, and I guess I won't be here long enough to make it worthwhile.'

'You could stay.'

She paused, her fork halfway to her mouth. She put it down. What was Max asking?

'Forget it,' he said quickly. 'That was stupid of me. Of course you have to get back to your mother.'

'It's a nice idea,' she joked. For it had to be a joke, didn't it? He wasn't serious. He'd said it on a whim. The warm, balmy air, the candle and the wine were to blame.

'Why did you come to Germany?' Max said.

Jo's eyebrows rose up. 'You know why. I came for Stella.'

'Is that the truth? Couldn't you have persuaded her over the phone to come home?'

Jo pushed her knife and fork together, her plate scraped clean. She grabbed her wine glass and took a generous sip. The ruby liquid slid comfortingly down her throat. Max had picked a quality red. She expected no less of a man who owned extensive vineyards. He was way out of her league.

Unexpectedly, she thought of home; the cramped semi-detached property with its chipped roughcasting and crooked guttering. There was never the extra cash or the time to get some jobs fixed. Inside it was homely and cosy, but it was never quite big enough for the three of them.

She came back to the present. 'Mum wanted me to come and get her. It was inconvenient, but I could hardly say no.'

'But you could have,' Max argued. 'That's much more logical than chasing your sister across Europe. A few phone calls and back she comes. Or, if she doesn't, what's the big deal? Stella's an adult; she can do what she likes. So what made you come here?'

'I . . . when you put it like that, it does sound silly. I guess I said yes to Mum because . . . because I was running away too.'

'And what were you running from?' His voice was a low whisper.

Something in the intimate atmosphere of the restaurant made her answer honestly. It was as if this night was special and only she and Max were sharing it. She trusted him, more than she trusted herself.

'I was running from decisions about my life. This thing with Stella has been a welcome distraction to making big choices about what I'll do. It was all wrapped up in what direction I take my business in and where I end up living. Then there's Mum. Well, you know how it's all turned out. I'm not moving out. I'll be staying at home just as I always have. And that's fine. Really. I'm happy with that.'

Max gave her a searching look but didn't say more. He didn't have to. Jo hadn't convinced herself either. There was nothing to be done. The decisions were made. *What if* played in her mind. What if she could stay in Germany?

'Do you want dessert?' Max asked. 'We can either eat it here, or I settle up and we get ice-cream from the parlour next door and wander around the city.'

'Ice-cream and a walk sound good.'

Max grinned. 'Great. Let's do it.'

The ice-cream parlour had almost

too many flavours to choose from. Jo chose vanilla and mint while Max had double chocolate. They took their cones and went out to the square.

'Where should we go?' Jo asked, licking the rapidly melting ice-cream from her fingers.

'Anywhere near the square is nice,' Max said. 'This is all the old part of the town. It's a city but it's very small, so it's more of a university town. That's why it's so lively; all the students socialise here.'

'Do you come here much?'

'I'm here quite a bit on business but I never come here on a day out. So this is nice for me too.'

'I've enjoyed our evening,' Jo said, wanting to thank him.

'So have I. Very much.'

They walked on until they found themselves on a stone bridge. Underneath, instead of a river or canal, there was another road and the leafy tops of trees. Jo leaned on the stonework and stared at the city. She felt Max's arm brush hers as he leaned there too.

'You complimented me on what I'm wearing earlier,' she said.

'It's a pretty dress.'

'I'm not trying for more compliments,' she said with a smile, 'but I wanted you to know that Petra made it.'

'She's clearly got talent,' Max said, sounding very much the proud father. 'I had no idea that her sewing was more than a hobby. It's difficult to tell with teenagers sometimes what's a dream and what's reality. And I don't get to spend time with her, so I've really very little idea what she gets up to.'

'But that's all going to change,' Jo reminded him.

'I hope Sylvie comes round to it. It would make everyone's life easier if we all agreed.'

'You'll make it a success, I'm sure. Besides, Petra's enthusiastic about coming to the castle and about the café. It's all going to work out fine.'

'You're a very kind person,' Max said, turning his head to her. 'A good friend. Thank you.'

'I haven't done much except nearly mess everything up for you, so perhaps 'thank you' isn't what I deserve.'

Then Max's mouth was hovering over hers, and Jo didn't have time to say anything else. There was a question in his eyes, and she answered it by leaning up until their lips met. It was the sweetest kiss she'd ever had. There was a tenderness, a strength held in check, as his arms wrapped around her and their kiss deepened.

They drew back at the same moment. Jo's legs quivered. Her mouth and her body begged for more. But Max stood back.

'Sorry, Jo. I don't know what came over me. I hope you don't mind.'

Mind? Please let's do it again. Jo shook her head at him. 'Of course I didn't mind, Max. I wanted that just as much as you.'

'Life's rather complicated now, with Petra and Sylvie. I'm not being fair to you by kissing you.'

She felt a rush of annoyance at his continued apology. It wasn't as if she didn't want his embraces. Or maybe he simply regretted kissing her. She pulled away from the bridge, the stone now cold to her touch. 'We have a saying in English. It takes two to tango.'

She started walking back to where they'd left the car. Anyway, she didn't care if she was taking the wrong direction. The cobblestones blurred as her sandals slapped across them. She just needed to get away from Max.

9

The next day, Jo still felt awkward with Max. They hadn't discussed the kiss. The drive back from Freiburg had been silent and their goodnights stilted. Jo wanted to remember their lovely evening in a happy way, but she couldn't forget the way it had ended. Nor could she forget the way Max's mouth had felt on hers.

She went in through the open doors of the café to find Max, Stella and Petra all waiting for her. Max and Stella both looked as if they hadn't slept well, while Petra looked nervous but excited.

'Ah, Jo, we wondered where you were,' Max said pleasantly.

It was if last night had never happened. If that was the way he wanted to play it, that was fine by her! She smiled politely. 'I'm not late, am I? I thought we'd need my laptop, so I went back to get it.' She waved it at him to prove her words.

'Good idea. Petra's brought her notebook too, so she can take measurements.'

Petra's delighted grin to her father made Jo remember why the meeting was important; more important than her own mixed-up swirl of emotions. Her shoulders dropped and she tried to relax. If she could help Max and Petra persuade Sylvie that regular meetings were a good thing, then she would.

Stella stifled a yawn. 'What are we doing?'

'When did you get in last night?' Jo asked.

'Before midnight. It was a fantastic barbecue and I met loads of people. I'm even learning a few words of German.'

'If you learn the language, you can have a job in the café.' Max grinned.

'Really?' Stella's face brightened.

It struck Jo that her sister wasn't as bubbly as usual. Maybe it was that she was tired, but Jo felt it was something more. She hoped it was because Stella was thinking about Andy. 'Don't be daft; you can't take a job in the café,' she snapped. 'What about your life at home? What about your job at Gav's? He won't hold your place for you indefinitely.'

'I don't care. Gav's isn't the only café in the world, obviously.' Stella indicated the room they were in.

'I didn't mean to start an argument,' Max said. 'Come on, let's sit down and get our ideas out.'

Petra took the seat next to Max. She opened the large bag she'd brought with her and spread out material samples on the table.

'These are lovely,' Stella said eagerly.

'Do you like the colours?' Petra asked Max, her fingers gripping the material.

'They're all very nice, but I'm going to need your help to decide what fits the café,' Max said.

'I'd say these are my favourites.' Petra selected a red and white diamond patterned cloth and an orange and yellow striped cloth. 'They are very cheerful and will make the atmosphere in the café.'

The young girl certainly had a talent for artistic design, Jo thought. She hadn't been convinced about the orange and yellow until Petra spread the cloth out on the nearest table and she could visualise it as a tablecloth. It would be bright and cheerful and summery.

'I like it,' Stella announced. 'I think you should have plain white crockery to go with it.'

'Or you could go for mismatched pieces of china,' Jo heard herself say. 'That's all the rage at home just now. Like in that restaurant Mum likes — you know the one I mean, Stella?'

'Clarry's, on Layton Road? Yes, you're right. It really works well; gives the place a . . . how would you describe it? An authentic feel.'

Then they were all talking at once about ideas and places they'd seen, and Jo realised the awkwardness was gone.

Petra fitted right in, despite the differences in age between them all. Jo was impressed that Max and Petra were able to converse in English out of politeness to her and Stella. It made her feel gauche, only knowing her mother tongue. How nice it would be to be able to switch effortlessly into another language. Perhaps she could learn German. Even Stella was learning, it appeared.

Her phone buzzed in her pocket. Excusing herself, Jo went out into the courtyard to take the call. It was Maureen.

'Mum, how are you? Is everything okay?'

'No, it's not. What's taking you and Stella so long? Isn't Max fed up with you yet?' Maureen's voice was querulous.

Jo's heart sank. It was as if a grey cloud had covered the sunshine. It was wrong of her, she knew, but hearing her mother brought back all the problems she was trying so hard to ignore.

'Max likes the company. He hasn't made any hints that we should leave.' She wasn't going to tell her mother how close they had come to leaving over Jo's mistake with Petra.

'It's been weeks since you left. I want you to come back.'

'I can't leave right now. Max is opening a café and I've promised to help. Once it's open, I'll be coming home.'

'I'm not feeling well. I need you here.'

'What's the matter? Are you sick? Have you got a cold?'

'I'm tired, and some days I can't drag myself about. I feel odd.'

'Have you been to the doctor?' Jo wasn't too worried. It sounded as if Maureen needed a rest rather than medicine.

'No point in going to Dr Wells. She'll tell me it's a virus. They don't want to give you antibiotics these days, you know. Or she'll tell me to eat healthily and do some exercise. As if that's going to help.'

'Well, I think you should go. At least she can rule out anything serious,' Jo said.

'I'm being silly, aren't I? I'd feel better if you were here.'

* * *

Max watched Jo talking on the phone outside, her slender back straight and her shiny hair glinting in the sunshine. His heart was in turmoil. He should never have kissed her. But he hadn't been able to resist the impulse to do so. The kiss had been everything he imagined it might be, and more. He longed to repeat it — even if Jo had looked daggers at him this morning.

He didn't blame her. He'd practically run away from her afterwards. But it was complicated. He finally had a chance to get to know Petra again. It was his one opportunity to get it right. If he did, then Sylvie had to see that it was good for their daughter. She had to come round. Max couldn't bear the alternative; he couldn't take being shut out of Petra's life anymore. Soon Petra would be legally old enough to make her own decisions about seeing her father, but Max didn't want to wait those long months through.

If Sylvie thought he was involved with another woman, Max knew she'd shut down the visits immediately. He groaned inwardly. The timing was all wrong. He wasn't in a position to start a relationship with Jo, however much he'd like to. Besides, where could it lead? She'd be going back to England in a few weeks' time. Or sooner, if what he had overheard was true. It sounded as if her mother was wanting her home.

'Dad, are you okay?' Petra spoke in German.

Max realised Stella had gone.

'She said she'll be back soon,' Petra said, guessing his thoughts. 'So we can have a chat until then.'

'How was your mother this morning?'

Petra rolled her eyes. 'The usual. She

told me I was making a big mistake coming here. That I need to concentrate on my school studies, and that being with you will confuse me. I'm glad it's the weekend. She can't stop me coming here then.'

'It won't, will it?' Max asked in concern. He didn't want to be the reason Petra failed her exams.

She laughed. 'No, Dad, it won't, believe me. In fact, it's the opposite. Being allowed to come here and help you with the café is going to motivate me to do even better in my exams. I want to set up my own business when I'm older. I'm going to make designer clothes and make a name for myself.'

Max felt an unreasoning rush of pride. His daughter was beautiful and talented and ambitious. He was a lucky man. Sadly, he couldn't take any credit for it. He had hardly been allowed to influence her in any way.

He should have fought harder. He should've taken Sylvie through the courts for access to the younger Petra.

Except that it might have made her life worse. If Sylvie was miserable and she and Max always at loggerheads, would that not have meant an unpleasant home atmosphere for Petra growing up? Max rather thought so, which was why he'd never pursued that avenue. Instead, he'd gone along with what Sylvie wanted. He'd trusted her and Pierre to bring up his daughter. They'd done a fine job of it. Only now, he wanted more.

Jo came back in and sat down. She stared at her phone with a frown, then put it away. Max wanted to reach out and stroke her hair from her temples; to ease away whatever was making her unhappy. But he didn't have the right to do so. Not after running away last night. All he could do was ask if she was all right.

'Yes, I'm fine,' Jo answered. 'It's Mum. She's not feeling well.'

'Are you worried?' Selfishly, all Max could think about was how he'd feel if Jo left.

'No. She's missing us, I guess. That's all it is.'

'If you need to go, I'll understand.' Why was he torturing himself so?

'We'll stay until the café's up and running. We promised to help. Mum knows we'll be going home at the end of the summer. She's trying to speed us up.'

He wasn't convinced by her laugh, but he nodded.

'Where's Stella got to?' Jo asked.

'She had a call too,' Petra said. 'She won't be long.'

'How do you go about making curtains?' Jo asked her.

Max watched his daughter's eagerness as she explained to Jo how the curtains would be carefully cut out of the materials, and how she then picked the design and made them up. It sounded difficult. He'd be all fingers and thumbs if asked to create them. It was a marvel to him that Petra could do it. If only Sylvie could see her right now, she wouldn't be able to deny how good this was for her.

'Tablecloths must be easy,' he said. 'They're just squares of cloth cut out.'

'No, you're wrong!' Petra said indignantly. 'It's very easy to cut the material incorrectly. Then there's the seams to stop it fraying. There's skill involved.'

'I never knew,' Max said, straight-faced. He shouldn't tease her.

'What are you two saying?' Jo asked, and Max realised that in her passion, Petra had switched to German and he'd answered naturally in that language too.

'Sorry, that was rude of us,' he said in English.

'Not at all. I wish I understood you. I feel very ignorant.'

'If you stayed in Germany, I know you'd become fluent quickly. Of course French is useful too, as the border is so close to us.'

'You speak French? I'm impressed.'

'So do I,' Petra chipped in. 'My step-father's French, so I learnt it really early on. As Dad says, it's useful for shopping over the border. Mum never learnt it, so Pierre and I use it when we want to have a private conversation. It drives her mad.'

Max should've felt jealous that Petra and Pierre had private conversations, but he didn't. He liked and respected Sylvie's second husband too much for that. And he was grateful to the man for loving his daughter like his own.

* * *

Stella pushed her way up through the vineyard paths. Her shoulders brushed the leaves and ripening grapes. The earth smelt warm and musty and sweet. She rubbed sweat from her forehead. What on earth did Uwe want? He'd phoned her and asked her to meet him at the top point of the vines. He was meant to be spraying the plants with herbicide, but he wanted to talk. She had no idea why he wanted to see her, but curiosity made her say yes.

He was sitting on top of a small tractor and waved as she struggled up the last stretch. 'Hi, there you are,' he said.

'Yeah, here I am,' Stella replied drily, feeling thirsty and hot. 'What's so important you had to drag me up here?'

He shrugged. 'It's not that important.'

'Oh. Well in that case, I'll go back to what I was doing.' Stella pretended to change direction back down the hill.

'Wait!' He jumped down from the machine, his macho stance vanished.

'I'm in the middle of a meeting with Max,' Stella said pointedly.

'You didn't tell him I phoned, did you?'

She shook her head. 'No, I didn't tell him you're skiving off.'

'Skiving? What does that mean? This word, I don't know.'

'Never mind; I'm joking. What is it, Uwe? What couldn't wait?'

He fumbled in his pocket and brought out a piece of folded tissue paper, which he held out to her. 'Here.'

'What's this?'

'Take it.' He pushed it into her hand. Then he stood, nonchalant, hands in pockets, whistling as if he'd no cares in the world.

Stella unwrapped the pale blue paper. It rustled softly as she peeled it. Within lay a gold necklace chain with a tiny crystal pendant. It sparkled as it caught the sun's rays. She gasped. 'It's beautiful.'

'It's for you.' Uwe didn't meet her gaze. Instead he seemed fixed upon his dusty black work boots.

Stella stared at it, then slowly she wrapped the necklace up and held the package out. 'I can't take this. It's too valuable. It's not right.'

He made no effort to take it back. 'It's for you,' he insisted.

'But Uwe, we're not . . . I mean, it's too much.' It was too much like a commitment was what she meant, but couldn't quite find the words to say so. She liked him as a friend but nothing more. And no matter what the problems with Andy were, the two of them were still together.

'I want you to have it,' Uwe said stubbornly.

Not wanting to upset him, Stella nodded. She slid the necklace in its pretty paper into her skirt pocket. Somehow, she thought, she'd find a way to return it without hurting him. 'Thank you, it's lovely. I have to get back now; they're waiting on me.'

He slung himself back up into the seat of the tractor with ease. His cocky grin was back in place. He winked at her. 'See you later.'

The necklace seemed to burn a hole in her pocket as she headed back. She was so conscious of it. Had she given Uwe the wrong message by accepting it? It was such an awkward situation. She'd tried to give it back but he wouldn't take it. What was she meant to do? If only she could ask Jo for some advice. But she knew her sister would say she shouldn't have taken it.

She had a sudden strong desire to hear Andy's comforting voice. Maybe it was time to go home. Her perfect picture of her German summer was unravelling at the edges. She'd just made a real mistake, her instinct told her, but she wasn't sure how to make it right.

As she grasped her phone, it rang. *Andy.* It had to be. Eagerly, she picked up the call.

'Hey, Stella — Gav here. How's things?'

It was hard not to sound disappointed. 'Hey, you! Things are great. In fact, more than great; simply fantastic.' She forced herself to be bright and cheerful. It was one thing to feel the shine coming off her grand adventure, but quite another to let others know it too.

'That's good, that's good . . . Listen, Stel — something's come up at the café.'

'Mmmm?' She was only half-listening, her fingers playing with the tissue paper and the shape of the crystal inside it.

'You remember Jonny Logan?'

'Jonny who got kicked out of college?' Where was Gav going with this?

'That's right. Well, his mum lost her job last week.'

'I'm sorry to hear that.' *What's it got to do with me?*

'So . . . I've given him a job at the café.'

'Gav, can we cut to the chase here please? Why exactly are you calling me?'

'I've given him your job.'

Now she was listening. The shock rippled through her. She'd thought she didn't care about working at Gav's café. In fact, half the time she didn't turn up or came in late, and Gav didn't mind. But hearing that he'd given her job to someone else . . . well, it was as if he'd slapped her. It was odd, but somehow being a waitress had been *something*. She wasn't good at it, but at least she had some paid work. Whenever Jo tried to prod her into thinking about the future, Stella consoled herself that she was employed. Now the rug had been pulled away from under her feet.

'You don't mind, do you?' Gav said. 'After all, you're travelling, and who knows what'll come of it. And Jonny needs the cash to help his mum. Are we good?'

No, we're not good, she wanted to shout. *What about me? What happens now?* A moment ago she'd been thinking of going home after the awkwardness with Uwe. But now she'd no job to go back to. As for Andy, she hadn't exactly been a wonderful girl-friend and kept in touch. Nor had she tried to resolve their problems — *her* problems. What if Andy didn't want her to come back? What if he'd washed his hands of her too?

10

There was a golden quality to the light as it was absorbed by the yellowing leaves on the trees. There was a cool sharpness to the air too. Jo sipped her coffee and watched a flock of birds wheeling across the sky. Behind her, Stella crashed about, making hot chocolate and muttering.

'Do you think Mum's all right?' Jo said.

'What?' The clinking of china stopped. 'Of course she's all right. Why wouldn't she be?'

'I just wonder if it's more than simply tiredness.' Jo had taken to phoning home daily to check on Maureen.

'You told her to go to the doctor, didn't you? He'd give her stuff to take if she needed it. Have you seen the cocoa powder?'

'Are you okay? You don't seem as

happy these days.' Jo turned to her sister. Stella was busy stirring the chocolate into the warmed milk. 'Stella?' she prompted.

'I'm fine. More importantly, do you think Max is okay? The grand opening of his café is this evening. Is it me, or is it a funny time to choose to open it? I mean, generally it's going to be a daytime café. Won't people get confused if they're invited for an evening event?'

'Why do I get the distinct impression you're avoiding my question?'

'Seriously though,' Stella said loudly, 'the evening?'

Stella wasn't sharing, that much was clear, Jo thought. Whatever was going on, her little sister appeared to want to work it through herself. Although slightly hurt that Stella didn't want to talk to her, in a way it was for the best. Some things had to be solved alone, and no one else could help. Like herself and Max — except there was no herself and Max; it was all in her imagination.

In fact, Jo wondered if Max had really kissed her that evening in Freiburg, or if she'd imagined that too. Ever since, he'd acted like nothing had happened; as if they were friends. So Jo was acting that way too.

'Well, I guess I'm talking to myself here,' Stella said.

'Max has made it clear that the grand opening is a special occasion, 'Jo said. 'The invitations have the normal opening hours on them. I hope it's a success for him.'

'Me too. He and Petra have both worked so hard.'

They took their drinks and went round to the café. Jo pushed open the door and they took in their surroundings. The colourful orange and yellow curtains framed the windows, and the matching tablecloths draped the wooden tables. Each chair had a similarly patterned cushion. Max had taken Stella's suggestion and bought in plain white china for the sugar bowls, salt and pepper containers and the tiny milk jugs.

'I spoke to Andy,' Stella said, lifting one of the milk jugs and setting it down again.

'How is he?' Jo kept her voice casual.

'Working hard, but he's got some leave due. He wants to come out here.'

'What did you tell him?' Jo straightened the nearest tablecloth and nestled the salt and pepper together.

'I told him to come,' Stella said simply.

Jo flew at her and hugged her hard. 'Oh, that's great. You two have worked it out. Well done.'

Stella allowed the hug before stepping aside. 'I don't know if we've worked it out or not. I told him to come because he refused to listen to any other answer. I've never heard him so determined.' She sounded surprised.

Good for Andy. Jo smiled. He was an easygoing guy, but everyone had a crunch point. 'But won't we be back in England before he's had a chance to come here?' she said.

'You'll be back in England,' Stella said.

'You're staying?'

'Since Gav gave my job to Jonny, I don't have to go back for work. If Andy's coming here, we can travel about until he has to go home.'

'And then? Surely you'll go with him,' Jo said firmly.

'I don't know. It's too far ahead to worry about. Let's concentrate on Max's event, shall we?'

'Well I'm here if you want to talk about it.'

'So am I.' Stella smiled cryptically.

'Now I'm confused.'

'No, you're really not.' Stella grinned. 'You and Max? Don't think I haven't noticed how you look at him.'

'Is it that obvious?' Jo said, horrified.

'Only to me, 'cause you're my sister. Besides, you and Max together — it's perfect.'

'Except he isn't attracted to me. We're just friends.'

'You shouldn't give up so easily. In

fact, how about I do you a makeover for tonight?'

'Stella, I don't — '

'Don't 'Stella' me. Let me sort your makeup and clothes and hair. Trust me — once I've finished with you, Max won't be able to resist.'

'Did I hear my name?'

Jo spun round, her heart leaping. She hoped he wouldn't notice her flushed face; that instant reaction to his presence. Her skin prickled at his nearness and her pulse raced.

'Jo and I were saying what a marvellous job you've done getting the café ready,' Stella said smoothly. Jo threw her a grateful glance.

'I'm nervous, I admit it.' Max grinned, coming to stand beside Jo. 'Tonight's the big night.'

'Excuse me,' Stella said, waving her mug. 'I'm going to get another drink.'

Then Jo and Max were left alone. Jo heard the electricity from the fridge hum and click. Outside, a flock of birds was twittering and the trees were rustling in the wind. She was all too aware of Max beside her, their arms almost touching.

'I'll be sorry to leave all this,' she said quietly.

'So it's true that you're going home.' Max sounded sad.

'I said I'd go after the café opening, and I must keep my promise to Mum. I don't want to outstay my welcome.'

'You could never do that. But you've been avoiding me, I feel.'

She risked a glance at him. His grey eyes were thoughtful as they searched her face. 'We've been avoiding each other,' she said.

He sighed and gave her a wry smile. 'You're right. Life's been busy, and I've been rushing about getting the café ready and spending time with Petra. I haven't been fair to you. I'd like it if we could spend a while together before you go.'

He wasn't going to persuade her to stay, then. It felt like a body blow. But she'd made it plain she was going, and there was no reason he had to ask her to remain.

'It was only a kiss,' she said. 'Let's not make too much of it.'

'Ah, there you are, Max.' They both turned to see Sylvie, with an expression like thunder. She insisted on speaking to Max alone.

Max watched as Jo left them. There was so much he wanted to say to her. He was keenly aware of how little time there was left. The café was opening that evening, and a day or two later he'd lose her. But what did he have to offer her? He had no right to ask her to stay. There was no future for them, not if he hoped to keep seeing Petra. Though right now, given Sylvie's fury, that wasn't certain either.

'How dare you!' she hissed. 'Carrying on with that woman while Petra's in your care.'

'Firstly, Petra's not here right now, and secondly, I'm not carrying on as you so nicely put it.' Max felt his own anger rise.

'You kissed her. I heard her say so.' Sylvie's body shook with annoyance.

'It's nothing to do with you. I don't interfere with your life, and you should extend to me the same courtesy.'

'It's everything to do with me, and with Petra. Don't try to blow me off, Max. You promised me that you'd provide a stable environment for her. I don't think that includes you having an affair with that Englishwoman.'

'You're being ridiculous. Petra's in no danger here at all. She loves it. Not only that, but she's done some great work getting the café ready. Don't you want to see it?'

Sylvie waved her agitated hands at him. 'Stop trying to divert me. I'm inclined to stop all this nonsense. I never wanted her to come here in the first place. So that's it; she's finished here.'

'Don't you think Petra should have a say in this?' Max said forcefully. 'She's not a child anymore.'

'She's not an adult either,' Sylvie

returned smartly. 'I'm her mother, and she'll do what she's told.'

'What will I do?' Petra said, stepping onto the terrace and looking just as fierce as her mother.

'Come along,' Sylvie ordered, grabbing her daughter's arm.

Petra slipped her grip and stood firm. Her dark brows, so similar to Sylvie's, were slashed in a vee. 'I'm not going anywhere, Mum. You can't make me leave.'

'You can't stay here when your father has a fancy woman. It's not right.'

Petra burst out laughing. Sylvie looked affronted, and Max wasn't sure whether to laugh or cry. So this was family life. It was far removed from his usual quiet ways. How did Pierre stand it?

'Really? You have a fancy woman, Dad? Who is it?'

'Petra!' Sylvie sounded shocked.

'Mum, I'm fifteen. Honestly, there's nothing to worry about. I'm not confused or upset. My schoolwork is going well and I'm happy here. I love you and Pierre, but I'm allowed to love Dad too, aren't I?'

Sylvie's mouth opened and shut.

'I'm not going anywhere,' Petra went on, 'and you aren't either. Dad needs me tonight for the café. We want it to be a big success. You have to come too and bring Pierre and all your friends. We need loads of people attending. Don't we, Dad?'

Both Max and Sylvie were silent. In a moment of solidarity, they stared at their daughter. She was so confident and strong-willed, and she'd said the right words. All the anger appeared to drain from Sylvie.

'I've never seen you like this,' she said.

'I'm doing something I love,' Petra said, going to her mother and taking her hands, 'I know I can make it my career. Please, Mum, come and see.'

She led Sylvie to the café. Max followed. He waited while Petra explained excitedly that she'd sewn all the furnishings, and insisted on Sylvie touching them and inspecting the stitching.

'You've made these very well,' Sylvie said grudgingly.

'Don't be like that,' Petra said, hugging her. 'Be happy for me.'

'I am happy for you,' Sylvie said, 'if it's what you want.'

'It is. I want to be with Dad when I can, when I'm not at home.'

Max noticed the emphasis Petra put on 'home' and was glad for his ex-wife. Petra was making it clear she wasn't leaving her.

'Very well,' Sylvie said, 'I'll come tonight and bring Pierre.' She made an effort to turn to Max and ask, 'Can I help with food or drinks?'

'That's very kind of you, but I've got a couple of girls from the village who'll bake cakes and biscuits. In fact they're going to work for me as waitresses.'

'I thought Stella was going to work in the café?' Petra said.

'She's gone off that idea.' Max

grinned. 'She's had a couple of bad experiences in the kitchen.'

'Jo's website's great,' Petra said. 'There's bound to be lots of foot traffic from the advertising she's designed.'

'I hope so,' Max agreed, 'but tonight is by invitation only. I have to know the numbers for the food and wine.'

'I can't wait.' Petra jumped from foot to foot and suddenly looked a lot younger than her fifteen years.

'I'll see you tonight,' Sylvie said. She kissed Petra's cheek and gave Max a short nod.

* * *

Max had one more thing to do before he got ready for the evening. He found Jo poring over her laptop as usual. 'Don't you ever stop working?' he joked feebly, sliding into the armchair next to hers.

'I'm booking my flight home.'

It took the air from his lungs in one rush. Struggling to recover, he could think of nothing to say. It was now made real — she was leaving. 'When?' he managed to get the word out.

'On Tuesday. That gives me a few days to get ready.'

'Right.'

'It's been lovely, Max. A much-needed break from reality. But I have to get back to my ordinary life. I'm worried about Mum, I've got clients I have to see in person, and now that I've decided to stay at home there's repairs I want to get started on before the winter.'

There were so many things he wanted to say, but in the end he didn't try to say any of them. Instead, he asked her what he'd been planning to ask before Sylvie had arrived.

'Jo, will you sing at the café tonight?'

11

'I changed my mind.'

'You can't. Now, hold still while I apply some of this smoky grey eye-shadow.'

Jo shut her eyes obediently and felt the light touch of the makeup brush sweep over her lids. 'What time is it?'

'You keep asking me that every two minutes,' Stella said. 'Chill, for goodness sake. No one's arriving before seven p.m.'

Jo did her best to relax. 'What are you doing now?'

'I'm using some of my best rouge to accentuate your cheekbones. Then I'm going to lend you my gorgeous new lippy and outline your lips with this lip liner.'

'Is this all strictly necessary?' Jo squirmed in the seat before Stella's hands pushed her back down.

'Yes, it absolutely is. Max is going to be stunned when he sees you.'

'What's the point?' Jo mumbled through the paintwork going on her face.

'Honestly, Jo, anyone would think you don't want Max to notice you,' Stella said with exasperation.

'But I'm leaving soon and he doesn't seem to care.'

Stella laid down her brush and put her hands on her hips. 'We do live in the twenty-first century with these things called planes. A great invention which allows long-distance love affairs.'

'You're assuming way too much,' Jo said. 'I have no idea how I feel about Max, and he hasn't declared any feelings for me. Forget it.' She stood up.

'I haven't finished,' Stella cried. 'Look, even if you don't want to attract Max, you do want to look fantastic for this evening, don't you?'

'When you put it like that . . . ' Jo smiled and sat down. 'I suppose I should make an effort.'

'Darn right. Let me finish your face, and then I'll show you the clothes I'm lending you.'

Jo felt the first twinges of nerves. Max had asked her to sing tonight and she'd agreed. She could hardly say no; he'd looked so enthusiastic. But it was so long since she'd sung to an audience. And her throat was dry. She coughed a little, hoping to loosen the muscles that were as tight as a band around her neck.

'So what's the plan for the evening?' Stella said. 'I didn't catch it all when Max was telling us.'

'That's because you were screen-watching while he was talking.'

'Andy was texting me. Turns out he can't have the time off he wanted because his boss is going to a family wedding. So he's coming out later.'

'Do you mind? Won't that mean a long wait for you?'

'A long wait in Germany will be okay. I'll get to experience the autumn here and maybe even the winter.'

'Don't you miss him?' Jo asked, curious to understand her sister.

Stella grimaced. 'Actually I do miss him, more and more. But it's awkward. I ran away from him, and now . . . well, how do I go back? It's simpler if he comes to me somehow. So I'll wait here until he does.'

'Oh Stella.' Jo sighed. 'Don't you see that you're running away all over again?' Stella's fingers flew to her throat and Jo noticed her necklace. 'That's beautiful. Where did you get it?'

She wasn't expecting her sister's groan. 'I didn't want to tell you, but Uwe gave it to me.'

Jo jumped up out of her chair. 'Why on earth did you accept it? Does that mean he thinks you and he are an item?'

'That's a very old-fashioned phrase, but yes, I think he does. It was just a really difficult situation. I tried not to take it but he insisted.'

'Of course he did,' Jo said. 'He wants to go out with you, and he wants more than friendship. Now you've encouraged him. You have to give it back.'

'I know, I know, but how?' Stella wailed. 'It's going to hurt him.'

'It'll hurt him more if you keep it and he discovers you already have a boyfriend. Does he know about Andy?'

'Andy's never come up in conversation,' Stella said shiftily.

'You have to give it back,' Jo repeated firmly. 'And soon. Promise me?'

'Promise. Can you help me?' Stella's plea reminded Jo of all the teenage problems she'd been involved in. She'd worn herself out helping her sister.

'You have to do this yourself,' Jo said. 'Do the right thing.'

'I will. Shall we look at clothes now?' Stella said, turning away to the heap of garments on her bed.

Jo was relieved to change the subject too. She wanted to help Stella, but her instinct told her to stay out of it. The sooner Stella confronted her own problems, the better.

There followed a half-hour of trying

on dresses, blouses and trousers, skirts and tops until Stella was finally satisfied with Jo's look. She wore a dusky pink jersey dress which clung to her curves. It had a scoop neck and short sleeves. Stella also lent her a pair of nude high-heeled shoes. Even Jo had to admit she looked good as she admired herself in the mirror. Stella's expertly applied makeup brought out her high cheekbones, and the smoky grey eye shadow made her eyes look larger. The lipstick brought colour to her face.

'You'll do,' Stella said.

Jo play-punched her arm. 'Hey, where's the compliment?'

'You look beautiful.' Stella grinned. 'Even if I say so myself.'

'That's fair. After all, it's all your work.'

'So what's the plan?'

'As far as I know, the guests will arrive at seven for welcome drinks, then Max is going to say a few words; and while I sing, the girls will be handing out the cakes. Then everyone chats, eats and drinks far too much, and goes home by ten.'

'Sounds great.'

'Yes, it does,' Jo agreed. But her throat was tight and her nerves strung out. She hoped she'd begin to enjoy herself once the singing was over.

* * *

Max's nerves thrummed. He could almost hear them, strung as tightly as the strings on his mandolin. He prayed he wouldn't be all thumbs when it came to following up on Jo's singing. She was to sing three or four songs, and then he'd play a few of his favourite short pieces to finish up.

He almost shot out of the café kitchen when he heard voices and a knock on the glass door. The two waitresses, girls from the village, giggled. They were busy arranging cakes and bakes on plates and garnishing them. They were doing a great job.

Peering in through the glass were

friends of his from Eichstatt. They waved and smiled. Max opened the doors, and a burst of chatter and laughter drifted in.

'Welcome,' he said. 'Please take a seat or wander round and have a look at the café.'

The waitresses hurried out with glasses of wine, and soon everyone was sipping and talking. Some sat in groups at the new café tables, while others walked around or took their wine outside, as the evening was warm and dry.

'Dad, we're here.' Petra ran up to him and hugged him. Behind her, Sylvie stood stiffly with a box of cream buns. She thrust them at Max. Pierre was beside her, looking relaxed and quite at home. It was a knack of his, Max thought with amusement. He wished he had the same calmness.

'Very nice,' Pierre said with a smile. 'We wish you all the very best of luck with it — don't we, darling?'

Sylvie cleared her throat. 'Yes. Good luck, Max.'

He didn't expect effusiveness from her; it was enough that she was here supporting Petra and accepting that he and his daughter deserved to be together. 'Come along in,' he said. 'Have a seat and drink some good wine.'

Petra took the box of buns and ran off to the kitchen. He heard her chatting with the two waitresses, who were not very much older than her. She was in her element. He was so glad she liked it here.

'Who's going to come to this café?' Sylvie asked, as if she doubted anyone would wish to.

'Hopefully the same people who come to visit the open rooms in the castle,' Max replied easily.

Pierre raised a brow at Sylvie and she flushed pink.

'It's only a summer café,' Max added, feeling sorry for his ex-wife. Her prickly behaviour stemmed from discomfort, he thought. She wasn't sure how to act when her husband and ex-husband were in the same space.

'You must be proud of Petra,' Pierre said. 'Sylvie tells me she's worked hard here.'

Sylvie had said that? Perhaps there was a way forward for all of them, Max mused. 'She's a credit to both of you,' he said honestly. He was rewarded by genuine smiles from Pierre and Sylvie, and felt himself smiling too. Petra had three parents and that was all right.

The waitresses brought out cakes and set them at each table. There were vanilla sponges, black forest gateaux, cherry cake, cupcakes, gingerbread and more. The sweet aroma of baking filled the café.

'Shall I make coffee too?' Petra said, arriving at Max's side. 'Some people don't want to drink wine.'

'That's a good idea. You can help Ana and Birgit make a few pots and bring them out. At this rate, I'll have to hire you as a waitress too.'

'Where are Stella and Jo?' Petra

asked, stopping mid-flight to the kitchen.

Max shook his head. 'No idea. Last I saw, Stella had lost a shoe, so it could be a while.' He glanced at his watch. They were on schedule, but he hoped to give his speech soon, and then Jo would sing.

He looked toward the door and froze. Stella burst in, a saffron scarf floating from her throat, her bright curls bouncing and male heads turning. But Max didn't see her; he saw only Jo. Coming in after her sister, she was a vision of loveliness. Her rose-coloured dress set off the dark glory of her hair, and he couldn't help but sweep his eyes over her slender legs. Her gaze caught his and he couldn't breathe. Then she smiled, and it felt so familiar, so . . . *right* somehow, that his heart clenched in his chest.

She came to him, and he smelt a delicate flowery scent on her hair. Her lips were glossy and eminently kissable, and he wished he could transport them both back to the bridge that night in Freiburg. He'd do it all differently. He'd do it better. No running away or making excuses. But it was too late. She wasn't his, and never would be.

'This is wonderful, Max,' she said. 'You must be so happy. Your café is going to be a real success.'

He opened his mouth, uncertain what in that very moment he was going to say.

'Speech! Speech! Speech!' A good-natured chant went up, and the guests thumped the table tops with their fists. Max saw Pierre wink and realised he'd started the call.

He put up his hands in mock surrender. 'Okay, I'm coming. Make way, please.'

* * *

The café was crowded; that was Jo's first thought as she went in. She was pleased for Max that so many of his friends and neighbours had turned out for his opening event. But it meant she was going to be singing in front of them all. Max looked handsome and relaxed, but she noted a tautness to his jaw which suggested he had hidden nerves too. She wanted to stroke away the tension with her fingers.

Her thoughts were so deep that she was missing Max's speech. She zoned in just to hear her name and see Max's wide smile in her direction. There was a round of polite applause. Max gestured for her to come up. She realised it was time for her to sing.

'And now my good friend Jo, visiting us all the way from England, has promised to sing a few folk songs for us this evening. Please welcome her.'

There was another round of applause. Jo took Max's place, with her back against the far wall of the café. She scanned the audience. There was Stella, grinning like an idiot at her and giving her a thumbs-up. There was Petra, a coffee pot in each hand, smiling. Jo recognised Max's ex-wife, but there were no smiles of encouragement there; Sylvie's face was stony. *Oh well,* Jo thought, *you can't win them all.* Weirdly, that relaxed her. She didn't have to please them all, only those that mattered. She sought Max. There he was, sitting at the back, his eyes intent on her. *I'll sing for Max,* she told herself.

She inhaled, filling her lungs ready for the first words of 'Scarborough Fair'. She'd start with her old favourite and then sing other ancient English tunes. She guessed they'd be new to this German audience.

Then something awful happened. Jo parted her lips to sing and instead burst into tears. In slow motion she watched the guests' faces look puzzled and Max rise to his feet, parting the crowd to reach her. She sank down into the nearest chair and covered her face with her hands.

* * *

She was in Max's arms, and still the tears refused to stop. She was vaguely aware of Max hustling her away into the café kitchen and shutting the door. Her throat was sore from crying and her breaths were shallow.

'I'm so sorry. I've spoilt your evening,' she said, rubbing her eyes furiously.

'Don't be silly. Let it all out, it's the best thing to do,' he murmured, drawing her closer to him.

She was secure in his embrace, the outside world far away. But she couldn't stay there forever. With a last hiccup of air, the flood of tears stopped. She lifted her head. 'I'm so embarrassed. What must everyone think?'

'All these people are my friends and neighbours in the village,' Max said gently. 'They're on our side, so no one's judging. Anyway, listen . . . '

On the other side of the kitchen door, out in the café, Jo heard someone talking and then a ripple of laughter.

'Stella's standing in for us,' Max said.

'She's entertaining the crowd. Soon they'll all be so involved with their cakes and drinks they won't notice us. You don't have to sing. Why didn't you tell me it was a problem?'

'Because I didn't know it was,' she said. 'I thought it was all right. I used to sing in the choir in front of audiences. Although it's been a long while, this isn't any different.'

'You never told me why you gave it up.'

His fingers were stroking her back. She really ought to move away, but it was so comforting that she didn't want to. 'My dad was my greatest supporter,' she said, trying to make him understand. 'I wish you could've met him. He was always jolly, never downhearted, a bear of a man. He could make my mum laugh even when she was in a grumpy mood. And he loved his girls, as he called us. He adored Stella; he used to carry her about with him in the restaurant and tell his customers how beautiful his little girl was.

'And he told me every day how much he loved me. He told me I was a star. He believed in me. When I took up singing, he said I had talent, and he pushed me into going to choir. I can remember being in the restaurant and Dad beaming at me and telling the whole place that one day they'd pay good money to see me sing in London.

'When he died, it was as if my whole world crumbled. Mum didn't cope. She spent her days in bed. I had to coax her to eat and to get dressed. Stella was so tiny that someone had to feed her, bath her and comfort her. I didn't sing. I couldn't. I left the choir and I never sang again.'

'Until I made you sing with me.' Max sounded troubled. 'I had no idea.'

'How could you have? I wanted to sing with you that day. I enjoyed it.'

'But singing with me is very different from singing here tonight. You should've told me it was too much to ask.'

'I wanted to do it,' Jo said. 'I wanted to help your opening night be a big success. But instead, I've had the opposite effect.'

He stopped stroking her back and brought his arms around her again. His kiss on her hair was as light as a butterfly's wing. 'You've shouldered your family's burdens for too long. You were fifteen when your Dad died, weren't you? The same age Petra is now. You had to grow up too fast and be the adult. It's no wonder you had this reaction tonight. The singing has brought back the memories of your dad and your loss. All that pent-up emotion, it has to come out sometime.'

Jo stared up at him. 'I never thought of it like that. I've always been the sensible one of the three of us. Stella tells me I'm old before my time, and she's right. I've had to be serious and take control. But lately, here in your lovely home, I've been able to let my hair down; to enjoy the summer and be a little bit selfish.'

'You're not selfish. You're a very caring person,' Max said. 'I've seen the way you worry about Stella and your mother.'

Their faces were so close. Jo saw the flecks of green in his grey eyes with surprise. She'd never noticed that before. His jaw was clean-shaven, and she caught the tiniest scent of a spicy aftershave. Did she make the first move; the smallest action to breach the centimetres of space between them? Or was it Max? Had he leaned just a little towards her?

It didn't matter, Jo thought, as their lips touched. She felt the heat and pressure of his mouth on hers, eager and searching. There was no need for explanations or justifications. There was simply the two of them. She let her fingers roam the back of his neck, feeling the crisp hair that curled onto his collar, absorbing the strength of his neck muscles. He held her tenderly as if she was delicate.

The oven made a sudden buzzing sound as the fan shut off. It made them pull apart. Max touched Jo's lips gently.

She pressed into him, needing his nearness. It was incongruous. They were having a romantic interlude in a café kitchen. She couldn't help but smile. Around them were prosaic everyday objects — oven, sink, pots and pans. It should've been roses and violins.

'That's better,' Max said. 'A smile is an improvement on tears.'

'You're not going to apologise for kissing me, are you?' Jo asked teasingly.

'No, I've learned my lesson about that. We both wanted it. So where does that leave us?'

'I don't know. I'm going home soon.'

'And I've Petra to consider. Sylvie's made it very plain she thinks I should concentrate on my daughter and steer well clear of romance.'

'Are you going to let her dictate your life for you?' Jo said with irritation on Max's behalf. Really, his ex-wife presumed far too much, in Jo's opinion.

'Of course not.' Max sighed. 'But I wonder if she has a point. Petra tells me she doesn't mind, but will it be confusing to her? Is it too much when I've only begun to get to know her? She needs my undivided attention, doesn't she?'

Jo shook her head. 'I can't tell you what to do. I don't want to confuse things. I'm very attracted to you, but we've both got very different lives in different countries. There's no future in it.'

They stared at each other. Jo was the first to look away.

'I want to sing tonight,' she said. 'I'm going back out there.'

'Are you sure? You don't have to.'

'I do have to. For me. Open the door please, Max.'

* * *

Jo's legs trembled as she stood in front of the café audience. When she dared to look around, she saw nothing but encouraging expressions. Max was right — they were on her side. Her first notes trembled but, as she sang on, she gathered depth and richness in the old song's melody. She knew it off by heart, having sung it a hundred times in the past. As she let the haunting tune take over, memories flew in.

She saw her dad, head thrown back in laughter, his big body shaking with mirth. She saw baby Stella perched against his shoulder, her fair curls contrasting against his dark shirt. And Maureen too. But a different Maureen. One who was younger and happier, no lines carved into her cheeks from pain and loss. Jo had forgotten how invigorated her mother could be, stirring the pots of tomato sauce, peeling garlic cloves and kneading the pizza dough; shouting *Davey! Davey!* to get his attention and rolling her eyes to Jo when he stopped in exaggerated surprise and then swooped in to kiss his wife.

There was a sweetness to remembering now. It was as if all the hurt, all the anguish, had faded, leaving only the good behind. The relief took Jo right up to the last whispered line of the song. She stopped. There was a brief pause and then the clapping started, loud and exuberant. She searched for Max. He was there at the back with Petra and Stella and they were all clapping like mad. His eyes caught hers, and the moment was so intense it sent a shiver right down inside her.

She wasn't allowed to leave. The audience begged for more. She sang three more songs before pleading to rest. The applause followed her as she made her way to the table at the edge.

'Well done,' Max said. There was a depth of meaning in those two words, and Jo touched his arm in thanks. He knew what it meant for her to stand up there. And it was thanks to him that she'd been able to do so.

'I still think they liked my stand-up comedy better,' Stella teased. 'Seriously, though, that was great. I'd forgotten you could sing.'

'You were like an angel,' Petra said.

'I wouldn't go that far,' Jo laughed. 'Anyway, thank you. This angel is desperate for a glass of wine and a big slice of cake.'

'The angel deserves it,' Max said, pulling out a seat for her.

Petra pushed a plate in front of her and brought a tray of cakes to choose from. Max poured the wine. Stella sat beside her, chatting about this and that. Jo sat in the middle of all the activity and felt fine. No, not fine. *Marvellous.* As if she'd been running a hurdle race and had cleared all the hurdles. She was surrounded by people who wished her well; people she loved. *People she loved.* Did that include Max?

12

Stella chose slim-fit jeans and a green and white checked shirt. It was cooler now, and summer was most definitely fading away. She pulled back her hair. She needn't worry about styling it, as Uwe was taking her on his motorbike for a picnic in the Black Forest. She picked up her leather jacket, a recent purchase from Sylvie's shop, and slipped it on. This was her opportunity to give the necklace back, and she knew she couldn't fail.

Jo was right; this was something she had to do for herself. It was tempting to try to persuade Jo to give Uwe the jewellery back and to avoid him, but she knew that wasn't going to happen. It was the reason she was reluctantly going on this picnic. Somehow she had to get the message across to Uwe that she simply wanted to be friends.

If she was honest, brutally honest with herself, she'd flirted with him. She'd never meant any harm by it — it was just part of her irrepressible, bubbly personality — but now she understood that she'd gone too far. She'd given Uwe the wrong impression. Now she had to set it right.

When she'd done that, she was going to phone Andy. She had to speak to him and had been avoiding it for far too long. She wasn't sure how the conversation would go or what she'd say, but it would come to her when she actually rang him. It had to.

She ran into Jo in the hallway as she went out.

'Where are you off to today?' Jo smiled.

'Uwe's invited me for a picnic up in the woods.'

'Isn't it a bit cold for a picnic?' Jo shivered. 'I've had to wear a jersey and fold my summer dress away in my suitcase. Just as well that Sylvie has her autumn collection in the boutique.'

'So you're really going home?'

'Yes, you knew that. My flight's booked to leave on Tuesday.'

'I thought you might change your mind because of Max.'

Jo shook her head. 'I can't wait here forever for something that's not going to happen. Max has stuff to sort out in his life and I don't want to interfere with that. And mum needs me too. Summer's over, Stella. For you too.'

Stella tossed her hair back. 'Not for me. I told you, I'm not going anywhere, except on the back of a motorbike for a bite of lunch. I've got to go.'

Jo called after her: 'Don't forget to give him back that necklace.'

Stella waved in answer and hurried outside. She didn't want to talk about it with Jo. Her resolve might crumble and she might beg for help with it. What a mess it all was.

She pinned on her brightest smile as Uwe appeared. 'Hi, let's go.' She swung her leg over the motorbike and got onto the seat behind Uwe.

The powerful machine roared into life, and she clung on as they zoomed out of the castle grounds and onto the country roads. Vegetation flashed by her, the yellows and burgundies of turning leaves and the corn hanging on the maize plants, dusty and ripened. They nipped in and out between tractors laden with produce heading to and from the markets. Everywhere in the vines, there was activity. Stella glimpsed people amongst the grapes: women with head scarves and overalls, men with pork-pie hats and denim dungarees. There was a sense of timelessness to the scene. This annual activity had been carried out in the same way for generations as the rich soils gave up their harvest.

After a while, Stella lost all sense of direction. They left the Kaiserstuhl and began driving up into the hills. The roads bent round curves and zigzags, and soon each side of her there was dark forest. No wonder it was called the Black Forest. The trees were so dense it was impossible to see any light in the undergrowth.

Eventually Uwe brought the motorbike to a halt high up on a grassy plain. The dense carpet of trees below them stretched for miles. In the near distance was a typical Black Forest farmhouse with a long, low roof almost touching the ground. Stella knew that this type of roof was designed to withstand heavy snowfall; she remembered Max explaining it. Just as traditional was the stack of logs against the wall of the house, from ground to rafter height.

She tried to imagine the harsh winter up here and failed. What would it be like to have to be self-sufficient? At home, she was used to popping out to the shops at all hours for snacks or magazines or makeup. She thought it was odd the people here had to rely on their own wood stack for heating. Didn't they have central heating?

'Come on,' Uwe said, 'give me a hand with the bags.'

'They're heavy. What have you got in there?'

'I told you I was bringing a picnic. That's the food and bottles of wine.'

'Is that wise, drinking and then driving home?' she said, alarmed. 'Is that even legal?'

He shrugged and didn't answer. She noticed his rigid back and realised she'd offended him. Great. She'd said the wrong thing already and hadn't even had time to talk about the necklace. She decided not to mention it yet.

'Thanks for inviting me out,' she said. 'Here, let me spread out the blanket and sort the food.'

She unfolded the red picnic blanket under his cold gaze and felt extremely uncomfortable. She reminded herself that it was only Uwe. She'd been out with him quite a few times by now to parties and gatherings. So what was different? As she took great care to lay out the plates and unwrap the sandwiches and biscuits, she realised what it was. She'd rarely been alone with him.

They'd gone with Uwe's group of friends to the barbecues and swimming outings and evening wine festivals. The only day she'd gone with him alone was to the dirty café the day he'd tried to kiss her. She hadn't enjoyed that day one little bit. Her heart sank into a pit somewhere around her stomach. She hoped it wouldn't be like that today.

Take control, she thought. *Stop being afraid.* That made her freeze. She was actually a tiny bit afraid of him. Why on earth had she agreed to come out here today? But she knew why. She felt guilty taking the necklace, and this was her way of making it up to him. Yet she suddenly knew she'd made a terrible mistake.

Pretending to focus on the picnic spread in front of them, she tried to assess her surroundings. It didn't look promising. Apart from the farmhouse, which was some distance away, there was nothing but countryside — green grassy fields and dark, dark forest.

'Shall we eat?' she said at last when

there was no more reason to fiddle around with the cutlery and the Tupperware.

'That's why we're here, isn't it?' he said sarcastically.

'Look, if you think it's okay to have a drink and then drive, then do it,' she said, hating herself for trying to appease him. 'It's just that in England we have very strict laws.'

'You think we don't here in Germany?'

'I don't know.'

'You don't know very much, do you?' He opened the bottle of wine and took a deliberate swig from it.

She watched him wipe the top of the bottle on his shirt and winced inwardly. What had she ever seen in him? He was a rude, swaggering, immature lout. That was the truth. She'd been flattered by his attention in the beginning when she arrived at Max's home. She'd basked in it because she was needy, and because she'd been trying to forget Andy. Jo was right — she'd done nothing but run away from all her problems. She wished Jo was here with her. She'd know how to handle Uwe.

Nervously, Stella picked at a sandwich. He was only a few years older than her, but he was so much taller and stronger. She thought about it. The best course of action was to have the picnic as if nothing was wrong. She had to look as if she was enjoying herself. She also had to make sure he didn't drink any more. Then — and she crossed her fingers here for luck — she had to wrap up the picnic as quickly as possible and get him to take her home.

She took a calming breath. It all sounded reasonable. Except she'd forgotten the bit where she had to return his necklace. She groaned silently. When should she do that?

'Aren't you going to eat that?' Uwe said. 'I went to a lot of bother to make this picnic.'

'It's delicious,' she said with a nod, forcing herself to chew and swallow.

Not a lot of bother, though. The sandwiches and biscuits were shop-bought; she recognised the local Eichstatt supermarket brands on the wrappers.

She managed to eat the sandwich and one biscuit, ignoring the plastic cup of wine Uwe poured for her. She had to keep her wits about her. There was a small bottle of orange juice and she drank it, the sugar giving her energy. There was no getting away from it; she had to talk about the necklace. She'd put it carefully into her jeans pocket before she left. Now she took it out and laid it on the blanket between them.

'What are you doing?' Uwe asked.

'I'm really sorry, but I made a big mistake accepting this from you,' Stella said. 'Please, take it back. It must've cost you such a lot.'

'I want you to keep it.'

'I can't,' she said. 'You see, I think it means different things to both of us.'

He looked suddenly younger and less sure of himself. 'I like you, Stella. That's why I gave you this. I want us to be more than friends.'

Nervousness fluttered in her stomach. The instinct to run flooded her. But she couldn't; there was nowhere to run to. She had to sort out the confusion she'd caused.

'I can't be more than friends with you,' she said in a low voice. 'I already have a boyfriend back in England.'

He jumped up from where he'd been sitting on the grass. 'Why are you telling me this only now?'

'I should've been honest with you from the start.' She pulled up tufts of grass in agitation. 'I was selfish and I liked the attention you gave me. But it was wrong of me. So you see why I can't accept your gift?'

Uwe's face was suffused with red. His eyes glittered dangerously. 'You lied to me.'

'I didn't lie to you. I just . . . didn't tell you some stuff. That's different,' she protested.

'No, you're a liar. You kept me around, spending money on you and sharing my friends with you, and all the time you had a boyfriend.' He made a sound of disgust.

Stella blanched. The way he put it made her sound awful. She hadn't meant for any of it to happen. Couldn't he understand that?

'I've apologised, and I am truly sorry. I've behaved badly. Can't we be friends? At least let's finish the picnic together and then go home.'

He moved towards her, his fists clenched. For a terrible minute, she thought he was going to hit her. Instead he lunged down and grabbed the necklace, stuffing it into his jacket. 'You finish the food,' he snarled. 'I'm going home. You can walk.'

Before she could react, he'd reached the motorbike, kicked the engine into life and driven off in a fug of petrol fumes. Stella sat there, stunned. She looked about. She was on a small island of red picnic blanket, the remains of the food and cheap plastic plates, cups, forks and knives strewn about it.

Beyond this tiny haven was nothing but grass and trees and the cold sky.

She pulled out her mobile from her pocket. There was absolutely no signal. The shock of Uwe's departure played over and over in her head. Andy would never have left her like that. *Oh, Andy.* What a fool she'd been! She'd had the love of a good, kind, steady man, and she'd left him without a backwards glance. All he'd done was ask her to marry him, and she'd run a mile. Many miles — to another country, in fact. Even after that, he'd been patient when she didn't want to talk about their relationship. He wasn't angry with her; he wanted to come and visit her on leave from work. She didn't deserve him.

Feeling the tears, hot and ready, pricking at the back of her eyelids, Stella pressed them shut until the sensation faded. There was no time for tears. Somehow she had to get back to Eichstatt. The only problem was, she'd no idea where she was.

Numbly, she gathered up the picnic

items and wrapped them in the blanket. Then she carried the blanket under her arm and began to walk towards the distant farmhouse.

* * *

Max was practising his mandolin when Jo came into the living room. The door to the terrace was closed against the rising wind. What a pity, she thought. She'd loved sitting outside in the evenings with him, talking and watching the stars and the homely lights of the village below.

He put his instrument down when he saw her, and smiled. 'I'm getting better, I keep telling myself. After the opening night in the café, I even felt I had some skill. But now I think my friends were being kind by applauding my efforts.'

'Not at all. You play very well,' she said. 'I liked those pieces you played at the opening.'

'It was hard following your marvellous singing act.' He grinned.

'It was a very good night in the end,' Jo agreed, settling down on the chair next to his. 'It must've been because it was hard getting rid of all the guests. No one left at ten o'clock, did they?'

Max laughed. 'No, despite the invitations stating when it was supposed to end. It must've been nearer midnight by the time we finished up. Still, that's a sign of success, so my daughter tells me.'

'I haven't seen her about today. Is she okay?'

'Yes, she's having a day in Freiburg with Sylvie. School is back now after the holidays, so she won't be around so much.'

'I'd like to see her before I leave. My flight's the day after tomorrow.'

'I can't believe the summer's over,' Max said.

Jo waited. If he asked her to stay — if he even hinted at it — she felt she might change her mind. She was going to miss him so much. They'd become such good friends. She'd never confided so much in anyone else. The sensation of loss was physical. She felt actual pain right over her chest bone, and pressed her hand to her chest to ease it. Like a bolt of lightning, she realised the truth. She didn't love Max as a friend; she was in love with him. As she bit her lip, she knew she couldn't stay if he didn't love her too.

'Yes, summer's over,' she echoed. 'What are your plans now?'

'There's so much to do in the vineyards this time of year. I'm hoping Petra will take an interest in it. Once spring comes, I'll open up the café for real, and I won't have a moment's rest. What about you?'

So that was it; he wasn't going to ask her to stay. What had she expected, really? She was no catch for a man like Max. He was a wealthy landowner and extremely attractive. He could choose any woman for his partner. Why would he want an average-looking brown-haired foreigner?

'I'm going to be very busy with my

clients when I get home,' she heard herself say. 'Then there's Mum to consider, and all the house repairs I want to get done. Like you, I won't have a moment to spare.'

'Will you come back to Germany?'

She glanced at him. 'I don't know. Would you like me to?'

He reached for her hands and held them fast. 'Nothing's changed, Jo. You know I can't promise anything. I have to look after Petra. I can't think about myself.'

She gently disentangled her fingers from his, ignoring the tingling his touch aroused in her hands. 'Then there's no more to be said, is there? We can't regret what we never had. You know I wish you all the best. I hope you get to know Petra, and that Sylvie accepts you, the way you want.'

It was as if her summer in Germany was already slipping away, fading out like colours seeping out of cloth into water. Soon Max would be no more than a warm holiday memory to be taken out and polished every so often. She'd think fondly of him and then go back to her everyday life, always wondering what might have been.

'Jo . . . '

She shook her head and touched his lips lightly to shush him. 'Don't say it, Max. Let's leave it the way it is. Let's be good friends, if that's all that's on offer.'

There was a noise at the door. They both turned. It was late now. Jo realised she hadn't heard Stella come in before. And there she was. Her curls were flattened by the damp winds. Her face was utterly white. Her jacket was muddy and torn and her shoes ruined by scuffing.

'What happened?' Jo cried, running towards her sister.

She was all too aware of Max's tall frame behind her, reaching out in concern too. Between them they held Stella, who almost fell into their arms. She burst out crying, and Jo and Max led her into the comfort of the living room.

13

Max wanted to go there and then and sack Uwe. His outrage was palpable, and Jo shared it. But sacking one of his workers wasn't the answer.

'It won't help,' she said as Max paced angrily and Stella sat huddled in the armchair, looking exhausted. 'He's behaved very badly, but he shouldn't lose his livelihood over it. Stella, what do you say?'

Stella raised reddened, puffy eyes. 'I don't want him to lose his job. Max, seriously, please calm down. You don't have to be angry on my behalf. Trust me, I got home fuelled by my own anger, but now I'm just tired of the whole thing. I didn't behave very well either, and I can sort of see why he got so upset. I just wish he hadn't abandoned me out there. I thought he'd come back, that he was giving me a scare, but he didn't.'

'What did you do?' Jo asked.

'At first I gathered up the picnic things and walked a little way. Then it struck me that he was probably being dramatic to punish me, so I sat down on the grass and waited for him. I don't know how long I waited, but it got very cold after a while. At some point I realised he wasn't coming back. Then I got a bit scared. It's not as if there are buses and taxis up there. In fact, nothing went by except a few cars going fast and one or two tractors.'

'So how did you get home?' Jo said. How terrified poor Stella must've been.

'In the end I walked across the fields to a farmhouse and knocked on the door. The woman who opened it didn't speak any English, so that made me a bit panicky. Anyway, she saw how cold I was — at this point I was shivering — and she made me a cup of tea and gave me a slice of cake. She was so kind. Then she made me sit in front of her fire. When her husband got home, I managed to make him understand that I was lost and needed transport. He drove me in his tractor to the nearest village.'

'And there was a bus there,' Jo said, nodding encouragingly.

'No, there was no bus. I hitchhiked.'

'You did what?' Jo cried. 'How could you do something so dangerous? Surely you know better than that. Anything might've happened. You could've been murdered.'

Stella rolled her eyes. 'You sound like Mum. It was fine, as it turns out. A middle-aged woman offered me a lift, but she wasn't going in the direction of Eichstatt, so she dropped me off at a junction. I walked the rest of the way, through the maize and in the middle of someone's vineyard, until I saw the castle. I've ruined my shoes.'

'I'm so proud of you,' Jo said.

'Proud? I thought you'd be angry that I messed up so badly. But proud . . . '

'Well, I am proud of you, so there.

You showed real initiative getting yourself home — didn't she, Max?'

Max nodded. 'Some of those Black Forest areas are very isolated. You did well, especially when you don't speak the language. But what about Uwe?'

Stella shook her head wearily. 'I don't care about him. I just want to forget the whole thing. Please?'

'Okay, I'll take no further action. But I'll be having a word with that young man,' Max muttered.

Stella yawned. 'Come on,' Jo said. 'You need your bed. In fact, we all do. It's very late.' She pulled Stella up from the armchair before she could doze. 'Goodnight, Max.' Jo hooked arms with Stella and guided her to the door.

Max followed them and paused at the foot of the stairs, looking at Jo. 'We need to talk.'

'We've said everything we need to say. You said yourself that nothing's changed, so there can't be any more to discuss.'

His expression was so sad that she

wanted to kiss him until he smiled again. But there was nothing she could say or do to mend their situation.

* * *

The next morning, Jo found Stella inside the café. The patio doors were closed and Petra's beautiful curtains were half-draped across the glass. Jo pulled the curtains open and let the light in.

'I thought the café wasn't opening for business until next spring,' she said.

Stella pointed to the kitchen, where Jo now heard Ana and Birgit's voices. 'Max has a group from Munich coming on a coach tour today. They want to see the castle's open rooms, so he's going to offer them afternoon coffee and cakes as part of the package. Birgit just told me.'

'Makes sense. Did you sleep well?'

'Like a log. I got an awful lot of exercise yesterday, one way or another.'

'I'm glad you can see the funny side

of it. Personally I'd like to see Uwe apologise to you.'

Stella waved Jo's comment aside. 'It doesn't matter anymore.'

'You've changed since you got here,' Jo said. 'I feel like you've grown up all of a sudden.'

Stella's mouth twisted wryly. 'For goodness sake, dear sister, I am twenty, not two. I think you sometimes forget that and go into mum-mode.'

'Okay, fair comment. But you have to admit, you have a somewhat . . . carefree attitude to your responsibilities. Or had. There's been a shift, definitely. You didn't run away from speaking to Uwe and giving him back that necklace. That was great.'

Stella went pink with Jo's praise. She may be twenty, Jo thought, but she'd always been young for her age whatever it was. Now she was showing maturity in her behaviour. Jo felt closer to her than she ever had. It felt more like they were friends, rather than the substitute-mother and daughter relationship they'd had growing up.

'Why are you in here?' Jo asked, straightening one of the tablecloths automatically. She hoped Max's coach party enjoyed the café and spread the word. She must remember to leave business cards with the café website's URL on them for the tourists to take away. That'd help Max.

'I've been doing a lot of thinking about my future. I got a real shock yesterday when Uwe abandoned me. It made me realise a lot of things.'

'Tell me,' Jo said, settling back in one of the chairs.

'Wait a minute,' Stella said with a grin. She disappeared into the kitchen, and Jo wondered what she was up to. A few minutes later she was back with two large mugs of coffee and a plate of cupcakes.

'Birgit said to help myself as there's plenty. So I did. Here, dig in.'

Jo sipped the richly flavoured coffee and selected a pink iced cupcake. She was going to miss Max's café. She was going to miss Max. She shook the thought free. *Forget it,* she told herself. *It's time to move on.*

Stella picked up a lemon iced cupcake. 'I wasn't very good at the baking side of things. I had a few disasters in Max's kitchen, which was a shame. I had this idea that I could do what Mum did in their restaurant, you know — make all the dishes and desserts. I had no idea of the skills and talent it takes. It made me see Mum in a whole new light.'

Jo laughed. 'Isn't that so often the way with parents. We take them for granted. It's a pity Mum doesn't cook nowadays. She might enjoy it.'

'She may get the chance to,' Stella replied mysteriously.

Jo raised an eyebrow. What was going on in her sister's head? She bit into her cupcake, tasting the delicious crumbly sponge, and gave Stella space to explain.

'So I had an idea and I came in here to mull it over. I'm rubbish at cooking, but I'm interested in the whole notion of a café or a restaurant. Despite what you and Gav think, I did actually like working as a waitress. And before you butt in, yes I know it doesn't pay well, but what about being the owner?'

'What do you mean? Gav's the owner,' Jo said stupidly, not following what seemed like Stella's rambling voiced thoughts.

Her sister blew out an exasperated sigh. 'I don't mean Gav's café. I mean my own. I've decided to go to business school to learn how to set up and run my own small business. Somehow it must be possible to get a loan to start a small café.'

'That's a marvellous plan,' Jo said, putting down her coffee mug and grabbing Stella's hand enthusiastically.

'It's a bit scary, imagining all the studying I'll have to do, but I know I can do it,' Stella said. 'If I have a goal to aim for, then I'll go full tilt until I achieve it. I can already see my own little café and how I'll furnish it.'

'That's the attitude,' Jo said, smiling. 'I think I see where Mum will fit in.'

'Yeah, I thought she could do the baking instead of me,' Stella laughed. 'And if she doesn't want to, then I'll hire in, the way Max has done here.'

Jo admired the confident way Stella was speaking. She could hardly believe it — her little sister was finally planning for the future. She was going to get qualified and run her own business. Who would have thought it? Stella's German summer had turned her life around for the better.

'I spoke to Andy this morning,' Stella said. 'It was hard, but I made myself do it. You were right, Jo — I can't leave it until he comes out here on holiday. It's not fair to him. I told him I can't marry him.'

'Oh Stella. Poor Andy.'

'I told him that I don't want to get married right now,' Stella went on, ignoring Jo's outburst. 'I want to be a student first. And then, once I'm earning, we'll get married.'

'So you're engaged?'

'I'm engaged,' Stella said solemnly, then spoiled it with a giggle. 'Oh Jo, you should see your face. You didn't really believe I'd dump Andy, did you? That was never on the cards. I was running away from the commitment, not the man. I've realised what an absolute treasure Andy is, having seen the alternative in Uwe. I'm not going to lose Andy to someone else. Not when I love him so much.'

'Does he mind not getting married just yet?'

'No. He's happy to be engaged for as long as it takes, apparently. He likes my study plans and he wants to help out with the café. Maybe I'll call it 'Stella and Andy's'. But more likely, I'll call it 'The Coffeepot' or some other cute name. I can see it now if I shut my eyes. Will you come and be my regular customer? I promise to give you free coffee just like Gav does.'

'And a cake discount?'

'You're pushing your luck. Oh, I'm so excited!' Stella squeezed her sister's arm. 'I want to go home right now.'

Jo looked at her. 'Are you sure about this? You won't regret leaving here? You were going to travel. Who knows what your future could be here.'

'Becoming a student isn't a whim,' Stella said. 'It's what I want. Now I have to make it and the café happen.'

The conviction in her voice convinced Jo. Stella was no longer running away; she was now running towards her very positive and exciting future.

Jo took the plates and mugs back to the kitchen. Birgit nodded her thanks. She was putting a wide tray of cookies into the oven, and they smelled fantastic. Jo imagined Stella running her own café, and perhaps Maureen doing what Birgit was doing now. It could really work. She'd offer her own web services to Stella to get her business up and running when the time came.

Max came running into the café, his

mobile phone in his hand. He stopped when he saw Jo coming out of the kitchen. Stella stared at him from her chair.

'It's Sylvie,' he said. 'She's broken her ankle. She wants me to run her boutique while she's off her feet.'

* * *

It was early evening and the Munich coach party had finally left. They'd had an energetic tour of the castle amid much noise and hilarity, followed by coffee and cakes in the café, which they told Max they had enjoyed very much. They were determined to make another booking for the following spring to see the castle gardens.

Max looked exhausted as he waved them off. The coach driver blew a horn, and the elderly tourists were herded onto the coach, all waving and calling back merrily. Jo didn't envy the driver. She felt her own energy drained by the afternoon. She'd helped serve up the coffee when Ana unexpectedly had to go home to her sick child. The castle was very peaceful after the coach drove off.

Max listened to all of Stella's grand plans and approved of them. He was going to be sorry to see her leave, but he was very happy for her. Stella in turn had thanked him effusively for his hospitality and for giving her a place to hole up, as she put it, while she sorted herself out.

Now Jo and Max were walking through the vineyard. It was a damp, misty day, and the spider webs glistened with dewdrops amongst the leaves. Max had invited her out for a walk. She sensed he needed to move while he sorted out his thoughts.

'There's so much to do,' he said, striding on ahead, then stopping to let Jo catch up. She hurried up the inclined path to him, brushing the leaves as she went past and making them rustle. Tiny birds hopped at the bases of the vines, darting for insects. Above them the clouds scudded across the deep blue sky. Goosebumps rose on Jo's arms. If it was chilly here, what was it going to be like in England?

'Can't Pierre run the boutique?' Jo asked, wondering why Sylvie needed Max to do so.

'Pierre has no experience of running a shop; he's an engineer. She's asked around their friends but everyone's busy with their own lives and careers. There's no one else.'

'Do you have experience of running a shop?'

'Not exactly, but I run the vineyard, the castle and now the café. It's not too different from those.'

'I can't see you selling designer clothes,' Jo puffed, feeling her breath catch as they reached the top of the rise. Gratefully she sank down onto the damp grass, heedless of it soaking into her jeans. She needed a rest.

Max crouched down too, with a deep frown grooving his forehead. 'You're right, I can't sell clothes. What was I doing, saying yes?' He ran distracted fingers through his hair.

'You were being kind and helpful to Sylvie,' Jo said, 'which is the right thing to do. But it does leave you with a problem. What about Petra? I've seen her in the shop; she's good at selling the merchandise.'

'I'm sure she is, but she has her school studies to concentrate on. I can't ask her to work in the shop.'

'You've got so much to do with your own businesses,' Jo said. 'How long is Sylvie going to be out of action?'

'The doctor said between six and twelve weeks for it to heal. It was such a silly accident; she stepped off the pavement when she and Petra were having their day out shopping, and fell. Now she has a plaster cast, and it'll be at least a month before she's back at work.'

'A month isn't very long,' Jo said thoughtfully.

'It's long enough, 'Max said with a humourless laugh. 'I don't know what to do. It was stupid of me to offer to help. I'm so busy.'

'I can help,' Jo said, her mind made up.

'How can you help? You're going home tomorrow.'

'I'll cancel my flight. I'll stay until Sylvie's better and I'll run the shop.'

'Jo, it's kind of you to suggest this, but have you any experience of selling clothes?' Max asked, throwing her question back at her.

'None at all. I'm not very fashion-conscious, as Stella would tell you. But Petra can advise me, even if she can't be in the shop. And let's face it, you need my help, Max.'

'What about your own work?'

'Another month away from my clients is all right. I do the majority of my work online anyway. I can work on my laptop in the boutique when it's not busy, and I can work in the evenings to make up the hours.'

'It's a very generous offer but I can't accept it.' Max rose to his feet.

Jo stood up too. 'Why not?'

'Because it isn't fair on you. You don't owe me anything for this summer. I've been only too happy to have your company. You'll never know exactly how much it's meant to me.'

Jo stood on tiptoe and planted a kiss on his cheek. 'I'm not doing it because I owe you. I'm doing it because I'm your friend. It's what friends do when there's trouble. They band together.'

'Then I accept with gladness. If you're absolutely sure.'

'I said I am. Let's not argue about it. I'm staying, and that's that. Until Sylvie's back on her feet. Then I must go home.'

'Very well, then. Thanks. I mean it, Jo. Thanks.' He gave such a huge sigh that they both laughed.

'That's all your anxiety leaving you,' she joked. 'The good news is, you can go back to being the boss of your vineyards and coffee *meister* extraordinaire.'

He gave her a sudden fierce hug. Jo's

arms clutched around him and instinctively she raised her mouth to his. The kiss was perfect, but he drew away.

'You're right,' Jo said, 'we can't keep doing that. We're friends, and we have to set a boundary if I'm staying here.'

'Agreed,' Max said. But he didn't look as if he agreed at all.

14

It was tougher than she thought, running a shop. She wasn't even 'running' it, if truth be told. She was on the shop floor, greeting customers and enticing them to buy the clothes, but Max did the accounts and Petra helped with the stock-taking after school.

Jo returned to the castle tired every evening. Max was working hard, too; it was harvest time, and the ripe grapes were being taken off the vines and transported to the wineries. There were still occasional couples and groups visiting the castle. Max kept the café open, and Ana and Birgit ran it efficiently.

When Sylvie's boutique was shut, Jo found herself taking her laptop into the café, to her favourite corner table, to work. Birgit brought her coffee and cake automatically, and she got through her client demands, sent invoices and built websites in peace. It was funny, but she quite liked it when there were a few other customers. The murmur of their chatter was background music and soothing to work to.

Working in the boutique was quite different. For one, she was on her feet all day and came home with aching calves and toes. For another, she had to put a welcoming face on when the door buzzer rang and someone came in — which was fine when she was in a good mood; but if her own work wasn't going well, it was hard pretending to be happy. The hardest part was selling the clothes. Jo didn't have a clue about fashion. She relied on the customers' reactions to the dresses, skirts and blouses, the handbags and shoes, the scarves and jewellery that Sylvie stocked.

Thank goodness for Petra. Jo was conscious of Max's concerns and never asked the girl to work extra hours. But she was incredibly grateful for Petra's tips and information about the boutique, and looked forward to the after-school hours when she'd arrive to help out.

Jo folded up a small pile of silk jerseys, stared at them and then unfolded them. No, they'd show better on hangers, she decided. She went into the back room and rummaged around until she found a box of wooden hangers. She felt the cool slipperiness of the silk as she hung them as precisely as she could. They came in an array of pastel colours. She'd hang them in a row in the order of the rainbow. Pleased with that decision, she hurried out into the shop with them.

Sylvie was standing there, supported by a pair of crutches.

'I didn't hear the buzzer,' Jo said, clutching the silk jerseys as if to ward the other woman off.

'So it would appear,' Sylvie said. 'You should be at the till in case a customer arrives.'

'Well yes, but I also have to keep the

window full of nice things.'

'Nice things? So you like the clothes?'

'These are lovely.'

Sylvie shifted uncomfortably.

Jo rushed to her side. 'Come and take a seat. How silly of me to let you just stand there. Are you okay?'

'I'll be better once I'm sitting. These blasted crutches, they are so tedious to use,' Sylvie grumbled. She let Jo guide her to the seats behind the till and moved gingerly onto one.

'I'm surprised to see you here,' Jo said. Surprised and wary. What did Sylvie want? Was she checking up on her? Jo supposed so. After all, she must be worried about leaving her business in such inexperienced hands.

'So your sister has left?' Sylvie asked.

'Yes, Stella flew home three weeks ago. I cancelled my flight and she got the last seat on the plane, which I'm sure was the one I let go. So it all worked out very well. She's missed the college placements this year, but she texted me yesterday to say she's got a job in a restaurant in our home town, which will give her lots of relevant training; and she's applied for college for next session.'

'And how's Max?'

Jo glanced at Sylvie. It was hard to read her emotions. Why should she care about her ex-husband? Then she realised she was being unfair. It looked as if she and Max and Pierre had all reached a consensus on how their family life played out around Petra.

'Max is working very hard. In fact, I hardly see him at all these days.'

'That's a pity. He likes you very much.'

Leave Max out of this, Jo thought. 'So why are you here? Have you come to tell me what a rotten job I'm doing?' she said, trying to keep an even tone.

'Not at all. In fact, the opposite. I came to thank you for saving the day.'

Jo stared at her in surprise. She hadn't expected that. Sylvie even managed a small smile. 'It was the right thing to do.'

'I know you didn't do it for me,' Sylvie said. 'You did it for Max.'

'Max wanted to help you out, but he didn't have enough hours in the day for his own businesses, let alone yours,' Jo said. 'You're right, I wanted to help Max.'

Sylvie made a sound.

'It's harder than it looks, selling clothes,' Jo said honestly.

Sylvie laughed, and for once her warmth reached her eyes. 'I'm beginning to see what Max likes about you. And Petra — she sings your praises to me.'

'I'm very fond of Petra. She's been a huge support to me. In fact, I doubt I'd have been able to keep your boutique open for you without her.'

Sylvie puffed with pride. It was the one thing she and Max had in common, Jo thought with a smile — their love for their daughter. Petra was a lucky girl to have three loving parents. 'How's your ankle?' Jo asked.

Sylvie smiled. 'You mean, when am I

coming back to work, don't you? I'm not yet four weeks in, and the doctor tells me it will about eight weeks to heal. But I'm coming in here next week if all goes well. That's why I came to see you today.'

'Are you sure you want to come back so soon? It won't be too much for you?'

'You can't stay in Germany forever on my behalf,' Sylvie said. 'Besides, I'm going crazy at home. It's so boring. Pierre is out all day at work, Petra's out at school, and I'm fed up with watching television and eating biscuits.'

'That doesn't sound all bad,' Jo said, grinning. 'Especially the biscuit part.'

'My waistline is expanding.' Sylvie shook her head. 'If I don't start work soon, who knows what size I'll be.'

'I'd miss my job if I had to have time off,' Jo admitted, 'so I can understand what you mean. You're right, too, about me — I need to go home. I'm missing my mother and Stella.'

'Won't you miss Max?'

More than anything in the world. But

she didn't say it. It was a private anguish, and she certainly wasn't going to share her emotions with Max's ex-wife. She picked up the silk jerseys and took them to the rack. Sliding them into place meant Sylvie didn't see her face when she answered. 'I'm very grateful to Max for letting me stay all summer. He'll be glad to have his space back when I've gone.'

'I don't believe that.'

The blunt words made Jo turn around to face her. Sylvie pushed up painfully onto her crutches and walked slowly across to the rack, where Jo stood motionless.

'I admit that I wasn't happy at first when I found out Max had two young women staying with him,' Sylvia said. 'I wondered what he'd got himself into. Then I was angry when you asked Petra to work at the castle. I didn't want her to see Max, for her own good. But Pierre is the better half of me. He talked me into allowing Petra to go there; and of course Petra is a very strong person, so I doubt I would have been able to stop her anyway. But now, when I see the changes this summer has made to her, I'm glad it all happened the way it did.'

'I'm glad too,' Jo said. 'This summer has been a turning point for all of us.' She was thinking of Stella.

'I'd like it if we could be friends.' Sylvie stuck a hand out while balancing her arm on the top of the crutch.

Jo shook it carefully. 'I'd like that too.'

Sylvie winced as she pulled on the crutches and moved her bad leg forward. 'Will you come back to Germany?' she asked, stopping at the door.

'I don't think so.'

'That's very final. Won't you reconsider?'

'I can't see a reason to come back. I'm going to be so very busy when I get home, especially when Stella leaves for college next year. There won't be time to go on holiday.'

'That's a pity.'

Sylvie fumbled for the door handle and Jo ran to get it. She opened the door and guided the other woman out. Sylvie's car was parked on the road. There was a woman in the driver's seat, glancing at her watch. She looked relieved when she saw them.

'That's my friend Marlies,' Sylvie said. 'She's been very kind and driven me around when I need to get somewhere.'

Jo opened the passenger door and helped Sylvie inside. She was about to shut it when Sylvie grabbed her arm.

'Goodbye, Jo. I may not see you again before you leave, so I wish you well. But remember, it's not too far to fly to Germany to see old friends.'

* * *

Jo got back to the castle after five p.m., ready for an early dinner and to sit down with a book. She wasn't going to look at her laptop this evening; it'd be a luxury to have a night off.

She'd barely fetched a glass of juice and a cheese sandwich when the telephone rang. Max was nowhere to be seen. Presumably he was out in the vineyards working. He often didn't get back until it was dark.

'Jo? It's Stella. I've got some bad news.'

* * *

The plane was crowded. Jo stared out the window, trying not to mind her neighbour's elbow digging into hers. In the aisle seat there was a small restless boy who kicked the seat in front endlessly. A harassed flight attendant rushed up and down, offering teas and coffees. Everyone looked as if they hadn't woken up yet. The early-morning flight was due in London at rush hour, and Jo was already dreading trying to get out of the capital to the hospital.

Maureen had had a mild stroke. She

was in hospital, where Stella had phoned from. No wonder she'd complained of being tired and feeling ill recently, Jo thought. She should've taken more notice of what her mother was saying. If only she could flick a switch and be at the hospital with them. The guilt bit deep into her. Poor Maureen; she'd been lonely with both daughters gone for the summer.

When she wasn't fearful for her mother, Jo's mind flashed to Max. She'd left in such a rush, after managing to book a last-minute seat on the flight. The short evening was spent packing up, and in the end she hadn't seen Max. She'd gone to bed early to get a few hours' sleep before leaving. At dawn she left a note and slipped out of the castle. Her taxi was waiting. She lingered a moment, looking up at the windows; then shook her head at her foolishness, slipped into the taxi, and watched as Max's home vanished from sight.

Her note had, of necessity, been

brief. She'd thanked him for all his kindnesses and explained why she'd had to leave. She promised to phone him that evening. But she wished she could've seen him one more time. She wanted to feel his arms around her, to soak in the heat of his body, to be enveloped in his comfort and security. But her German summer was over.

She bought a coffee from the flight attendant. The man beside her passed it carefully over his son's head to her and they shared a smile. It was a small kindness that almost made her cry; her emotions were so close to the surface right now. Jo sipped the hot liquid. Outside, the sky was an intense blue and the sun's rays shone like the petals of a flower. Below was a carpet of pillowy clouds. She gazed unseeingly at it all. She'd never see Max again.

It hammered into her chest: she'd lost him. Would he miss her? Right now it was as if there was a gaping hole where her heart should be. Something precious and essential had been ripped away, and going home felt hollow. She'd left her happiness in Germany.

* * *

Max stared hard at the stack of papers in front of him. With a sigh, he pushed them away. It was a week since Jo had left and he still couldn't concentrate on his accounts. If only he'd seen her before she'd gone. One last sight of her. It wasn't much to ask, was it? He rubbed at his face and the stubble on his chin rasped. It was a busy season in the vineyards. In one way that was a blessing, as he couldn't dwell on what might have been during the day when he was working so hard. But it also meant he hadn't had a moment to come to terms with the fact that he'd lost her.

He got up and went downstairs to pour a glass of wine. It reminded of him of the many evenings he'd enjoyed with Jo, sitting and chatting about various subjects. He'd never been so honest and open with anyone. It was as if they were children again, sharing their innermost thoughts. He was totally at ease with her.

As he reached for a glass, his fingers halted. He was kidding himself. Jo wasn't simply a friend. He was in love with her. There it was — the truth that had been hovering just out of sight for weeks. He loved everything about her. She was pretty and amusing, interesting and kind, generous and tender.

And what was he going to do about it? Nothing. Could he really put his own happiness before the stability that Petra needed? He groaned.

The doorbell rang and rang. He frowned. He wasn't expecting anyone this evening. Whoever it was, they were very persistent. He was tempted not to answer, but the ringing was annoying. He went to the door. It was Sylvie.

'Aren't you going to invite me in?' she said when he made no move to do so. 'Pierre's waiting for me in the car outside. This won't take long.'

'Yes, of course. Come in. I'm surprised to see you, that's all.' He led the way back to the kitchen. 'Will you join me in a glass of wine?'

'I hope you're not drinking too much on your own?'

'Why would I?'

'Because Jo's gone.' Sylvie took a seat at the kitchen table without waiting to be asked. She propped her crutches beside her. 'How are you, Max?'

He sat opposite her and concentrated on pouring the good red wine into two stemmed glasses.

'Max?' she prompted.

He pushed a glass over to her. '*Prost*.'

'What are we drinking to?' When he didn't answer, she sighed deeply and held his gaze. 'We were very young, weren't we? We should never have got married.'

He smiled. 'We thought we were in love. That was enough.'

'But it wasn't enough,' she said, 'and we were too young to know what true love is. We ended up hurting each other instead.'

'I regret that. All the arguments and the tension. But I don't regret having Petra. She's the best of both of us.'

'Yes, she is.' Sylvie gave him a smile with a tinge of sadness. 'I haven't been very fair to you. I'm sorry that I didn't let you have more contact with Petra when she was growing up.'

'I understood your reasoning and I agreed with it,' Max said. 'You don't need to apologise.'

'I think I do. I did it for all the wrong reasons.' Sylvie's hands tightened on the stem of the glass. 'You see, I . . . I was scared of losing her. I thought that if . . . if she lived half with you and half with me, one day she might choose between us, and I'd be the loser. I couldn't bear the idea of not being with her every day, so I forced you to lose out. I'm ashamed of myself.'

'Sylvie,' Max said gently, putting his hands over hers, 'it's okay. I understood all that a long time ago. And I accepted it was for the best, for Petra's best. You and Pierre have given her a loving home and two great parents. Look how she's turned out. She's a great girl, with lots of ambition and positive energy. She's doing well at school and she's got plenty of friends. It's all turned out well.'

'But what about you? You missed out and it's my fault. Seeing how happy Petra is these days, spending the hours here with you and at the café, made me realise what she's been missing out on too.'

'Let's leave the past behind. The present is pretty good, and the future looks bright too. Come, Sylvie, let's move on. I'd like it if we could be friends.'

'To being friends.' She raised her glass.

Max clinked his glass to hers and they both sipped as a bond was made.

'Have you heard from Jo?' Sylvie asked.

'A telephone call. Her mother has

made a full recovery, thank goodness. She had swift treatment, which apparently makes all the difference to the outcome of a stroke. She's back home and taking it easy. Jo's looking after her and Stella too.'

'You miss her.'

'She's a good friend.'

Sylvie shook her head. 'Don't bother to hide it. I can see you're in love with her. Anyone can.'

'Is it that obvious? I only just worked it out myself.'

'The night of the café opening, you couldn't take your eyes off her. Petra remarked on it, and she was right.'

'I promised you to put Petra first, and I have. You're right, it's important that she has stability in her life.'

'Petra's more mature than either of us realise.' Sylvie smiled. 'Who do you think sent me up here tonight to talk to you?'

'I don't understand.'

'Petra's worried about you; she says you look sad every day. She wants you to ask Jo to come back. And so do I. You deserve your happiness, Max.'

When Sylvie left, Max put the bottle of wine away and rinsed out the glasses. A hard knot had eased in his chest. Sylvie had opened the way for him to have everything he wanted: access to Petra, a friendship with his ex-wife and Pierre, and most of all, the removal of the barrier to loving Jo.

The question was, if he asked . . . would she come back?

15

The rain trickled down the back of Jo's neck. She sheltered in a doorway, waiting for the downpour to stop. It was one of those October days when it never really got light. Although it was midday, it could easily have been mistaken for evening. Cars flashed by, their red and white lights brightening the gloom. The spray from them misted the air and the drain water gurgled along the side of the pavement.

She'd just spent an unhappy two hours with a disgruntled client. He hated the website she'd created for him; it was nothing like what he'd described to her originally. Hadn't she listened to a word he'd said? What about all the emails he'd bombarded her with? Hadn't any of that sunk in?

The problem was, he was right; the website was mediocre. She should've done better. Somehow she couldn't raise the level of enthusiasm she needed to make it sparkle. All his email instructions had failed to click with her. She was distracted, and these days it often felt as if her head was full of cotton wool. Her nose was stuffed up; she was sure she had a cold coming on. But that wasn't the reason.

It was as if the summer had never been. Had she actually soaked in the hot sunshine on Max's terrace? It seemed impossible, as did Max himself. Their kisses, their hugs, their conversations . . . all those precious moments with him. They'd gone, and it was painful to realise they weren't coming back. Max didn't need her; he was busy with his life. So where did that leave Jo?

She should be busy with her own life. But, like her client's website, she just couldn't summon up the energy to deal with it. She'd always had an important goal to aim for: bring Stella up properly, set up her own business, look after Maureen. Well she'd done her best for Stella, who no longer needed her. Her business, though currently slightly rocky, was basically okay. That left Maureen. Jo was caring for her mother, but it wasn't enough. There was a huge hole in Jo's life, a hunger for something just out of reach. The days, months and years stretched ahead of her without anticipation.

Snap out of it, she told herself. The rain eased a little. She put her laptop bag over her head as a makeshift hat and stepped out into the street. Flagging down a taxi, she gave her home address. Then, as the taxi took the corner way too fast, sending a spray of dirty water up at the passing pedestrians, she changed her mind. She leaned forward and gave other directions.

Gav's café was a beacon of light in the square. Outside, it was dull and drizzly, but through the window there were warm lamps, flickering candles in pots on the tables, and people drinking coffee, hunched over their cups getting warm.

She pushed open the door, hearing the familiar jangly tune of the bell. Gav, a tea towel draped over one shoulder and the phone crooked into his neck, waved at her. Jo waved back and found a small corner table. Lizzie came over.

'Hi, Jo. What can I get you?'

'A pot of coffee and whatever the cake of the day is, please.'

'It's apple cake today. That okay?'

Jo nodded and Lizzie sped off, pencil twisted into her hair to keep it up, her black waitress uniform neat and her heels clacking. She rested back in the chair, fighting fatigue. Maureen was often up in the night, and Jo would wake at the sound of the kettle being boiled at two a.m. or so. She'd hear her mother wandering around the house or the low muted murmur of the television downstairs. It took hours to get back to sleep. Her alarm, going off at seven, was a daily shock.

A cup slid onto the table amid the

clatter of a coffee pot and plates. The aroma of warm, spicy apples and sweet crumble made her look up.

Gav grinned. 'Hey, good to see you.' He slid into the chair opposite. 'How's things?'

'Never better,' Jo lied with a smile.

'Try again.' Gav stared at her. 'You look awful. What's up?'

'Thanks,' she laughed. 'That's just what I wanted to hear.'

'Spit it out. Is it Stella? Is she still giving you grief?'

Jo poured two cups of coffee and pushed one over to him. 'Stella is amazing. She's the one part of my life that's going well. She loves her job at Clarry's, and she's learning so much. I don't see much of her these days. She's either working in the restaurant or spending her evenings with Andy.'

'That's good. She finally sorted herself out.' Gav grinned. He cut the wedge of apple cake expertly into two slices and offered one to Jo. 'I knew she would, eventually. Like a barrel of whisky.'

'What?'

'A barrel of whisky. Takes a whole lot of time to mature, but it's worth the wait.'

'It's an odd expression, but yes, very true of Stella. She's more sorted out than me, which is ironic.'

'Ah . . . I recall you met someone in Germany. What happened?'

'How did you . . . ? I guess Stella told you about Max.'

Gav nodded and took a great gulp of coffee, then topped up Jo's cup and settled back in the chair.

'Don't you have to serve the customers or run the till?' Jo plucked at her paper napkin.

'Nope. Lizzie's doing a fine job, and I've finally trained Jonny to take in the cash and print out receipts. So I'm all yours, and I'm all ears.'

'There's nothing to tell,' Jo sighed. 'I met Max, and we got along well, and now . . . I'm back here and have to get on with my life.'

'That sounds awful.'

She glanced up from her plate of crumbs to see if he was being sarcastic. Instead, she saw sympathy on his usually cheerful face. Tears threatened, and she squeezed her eyes shut to stop them. 'I'm fine. Or I will be. Besides, Mum needs me.'

'Stella told me that Maureen made a full recovery, and that she wasn't at risk of further strokes. Are you so sure she needs you?'

'She's upset and frightened about what happened. She's worried in case she does have another, despite what her doctor's told her. I can't leave her on her own too much. I tend to work in the living room now, where she's sitting, instead of my home office.'

'That can't be easy, trying to get your work done like that.'

'No, it's not. But what else can I do?' Jo asked with a helpless shrug.

'Tough love? Move out, get your own place, and pop in on Maureen each day. Got to be healthier than the way you're living now.'

'I can't do that, Gav. It's too cruel. No, I'll have to get used to it. This is the way things are now, and I have to accept that.'

Gav stared searchingly at her. 'A piece of advice, freely given. Don't live to have regrets. Don't wake up one day to discover that you let it all fly past and you made no good memories.'

Jo drained the last of the cup and stood up. 'I've got to go. Thanks for the chat.'

Gav stood too. He waved Jo's money away. 'My treat. Think about what I said. Promise?'

'Promise. Sorry, I should've asked about the wedding. I'm looking forward to it. How's Phil?'

'He's as excited as I am. The cake's made, the photographer's booked, and the wedding organiser is pulling her hair out over all the details. But we're good to go, next Saturday. Did you get your invite?'

'On beautifully thick paper that must've taken a couple of trees to make.'

Gav laughed. 'Yeah, nothing but quality for our nuptials. I'll see you then.'

* * *

Jo let herself into the house. It was dark and chilly. She flicked the switch on the central heating and the radiators rattled into life.

'Mum?' she called, going through to the kitchen, putting on the lights as she went. Maureen was sitting in the dark room, staring out into the garden. Rain trickled down the window.

'Why are you in here? Aren't you cold?' Jo had a sudden horrible memory of the bad old days when Maureen couldn't get out of bed and it was up to herself to get the house warm and get Stella up and dressed.

'I've just come in the door.'

'So that's why the heating and the lights were off?'

'No point having the heating on if I was going out and you were out too,' Maureen said. 'I should've put the lights on, but my mind was on other things. Sorry, love.'

'Are you okay?' Jo asked. It was unlike her mother to go out of the house.

Maureen turned to her. 'Jo, can you do me a favour?'

'Of course — anything. What is it?'

'I want to go back out. Will you come with me?'

Jo shivered and glanced out at the rain and the navy-streaked sky. 'You want to go out in that? Where would we go?'

'Do you remember the bay?'

'Where we used to go as a family for picnics on the beach?'

'Yes, that's the one. I want to drive there.'

Jo looked at her. There was no agitation or sign of confusion, yet it was an odd request. The bay was a few villages away on the coast. It was a sheltered area of yellow sands and shallow sea. As kids, she and Stella had roamed it, gathering shells and sticks and returning to the picnic their parents laid on. She had many memories, before Stella was born, of going there with her mum and dad for a day out. A day which, in her mind, always finished with a fish-and-chip supper. She could almost smell the salt and vinegar and the tang of the sea.

'All right, Mum. Let me get your coat for you; it's freezing out there. And I want a jumper and a scarf. Give me a minute to get ready.'

* * *

Jo drove carefully along the country lanes towards the bay. There wasn't much traffic, but the rain slicked the windscreen and there were occasional flooded areas. A lorry drove past in a screech of wheels. Jo's heart leapt as she steered too close to the hedge and branches scratched on the windows like fingers down glass. It was a relief to turn into the small car park overlooking the bay. She turned the engine off.

'What's this all about, Mum?' she asked, turning to face Maureen in the passenger seat.

'Wait,' Maureen said, holding her palm up for silence.

Jo waited, but there was nothing; simply the pitter-patter of raindrops on the windscreen and the distant roar of the sea far out in the bay. The beach, down below them, was a vast space of yellow sand with a tideline of seaweed in a curving brown strip. Gulls, crying on the wind, sounded sad with their keening.

'Davey and I loved this place,' Maureen said quietly. 'We brought you girls here as much as we could. It wasn't easy getting away from the restaurant — we were always so busy — but your dad was determined we'd have our days out.'

'I remember them well,' Jo said. 'We were so excited, getting bundled into the car with our buckets and spades, looking forward to ice-creams from the stall right here at the edge of the car park. One year there was donkey rides. Or did I make that up?'

Maureen laughed. 'You didn't imagine it. You're right, there were donkeys. That was a lovely surprise. Stella was too small to ride, but you did, up and down the beach until we had to pay the man extra and then persuade you to come off the poor animal.'

'Dad used to let us cover him up with sand, and then he'd leap out growling and we'd scream and run into the sea. We had so much fun.'

There was a moment of silence. Jo risked a glance at her mother. Was it all too much, raking over the old memories? But Maureen's face was peaceful as she looked out at the bay.

'You didn't ask me where I went today,' she said to Jo.

'I didn't want to be nosey.'

'I visited Frankie.'

Frankie was Jo's Dad's sister, who lived an hour away in a small town. Jo knew she and Maureen kept in touch, but they rarely saw each other.

Maureen clasped Jo's hand. 'You're unhappy, my love, and I'm to blame.

Something has to change. In fact, *I* have to change. I've been carrying my guilt for far too long. I want to apologise to you for not being there when you were growing up.'

'You were there, Mum,' Jo protested.

Maureen shook her head. 'You know what I mean. I was mourning for so long, and I forgot that you and Stella were too. I let my own problems swamp me and you paid the price. You looked after Stella and me, all at such a young age. I admire you and I wish I had your strength.'

'It's what families do. We look after each other.'

'Yes, and now it's my turn to look after you. You've been miserable since you got back from Germany. And it's all my fault.'

'It's not your fault that you had a stroke, Mum. No one could've predicted that. And I'm glad I can look after you.'

Maureen's grip on Jo's hand tightened. 'I've been very selfish. I wanted you to stay at home with me and keep me company. You know I'm not good on my own; I feel so lonely. Then with the stroke, there was a reason to keep you with me. But I had another visit to the doctor, and she was quite blunt. She said I'm as fit now as I was before the stroke, and I have to get up and get on with life, as she put it. I don't need you to nurse me, Jo.'

'There's no harm in wanting company,' Jo said, using both her hands to warm Maureen's in the cooling interior of the car. 'I can live at home with you. I want to, although I'm glad you've been given a clean bill of health.'

'Go to him,' Maureen said. 'Go back to Germany and see if there's a future there for you. And if it doesn't work out, you can come back and buy your flat and start your life properly.'

'Mum . . . ' Jo said, but she couldn't manage another word.

'I had my Davey, and I loved that man. If you found a love like that, I'd be content. I feel that Stella has got that love with Andy. Thank goodness she came to her senses and returned to him. I don't see her running away from her problems again. I want you to be happy now, too, love.'

'I can't go back,' Jo cried. 'What if Max doesn't feel the same way about me?'

'You'll never find out if you don't ask.'

'If he loved me, he'd come over here to find me.'

'Or, like as not, he's sitting away over there in Germany saying exactly the same thing to himself. Someone's got to make the first move.'

'I'll think about it,' Jo said finally when Maureen stayed quiet.

A gust of wind blew strings of rain onto the car. Out at sea, white foam skimmed the waves. The sea was black ink and the winds whipped it up. Sand grains spiralled up from the beach. Inside the car, the air chilled. Jo turned on the engine and put the heater on high. In a moment the warmth hit their feet.

'I'll go after Gav's wedding,' she said, not certain if she meant it.

Maureen let Jo's hand go and slipped on her gloves. 'The thing is, love, I went to see Frankie for a reason. She's a widow too, and has that huge house to maintain. She suggested I move in with her. With two of us to look after the house, it'll be much easier. And we'll be company for each other. She's even got some brochures; we're thinking we could take a cruise next summer to Egypt or the Med. I'm going to sell the house and use the money to travel and pay my way at Frankie's.'

'You're selling the house?'

Maureen nodded. 'I plan to give you some money towards a flat and some to Stella for her college studies. But I'm not giving you yours until you've been to Germany and spoken to Max.'

Jo stared at her mother. Maureen laughed and pulled her into a hug. Jo felt the comfort of her mother's arms.

16

'Champagne, darling?' Stella handed Jo a flute full of fizzing liquid and stood beside her, surveying the guests. She was dressed in a crimson silk skirt and strappy top, which accentuated her neat figure. On her blonde curls perched a hat with a jaunty feather. Her engagement ring sparkled in the light from the chandeliers.

Jo felt rather underdressed by comparison. She'd chosen a velvet dress of dark blue with gold thread shot through it, and definitely no hat. Her hair was swept up into a French twist, and she wore a tiny pearl-drop earring in each ear. It wasn't as if she was out to impress, she thought.

Gav and Phil's wedding reception was being held in an old English manor house that dated back to the 1700s and was surrounded by glorious autumn woodlands and sweeping lawns. The weather had been kind, and the day was one of bright blue skies, sharp sunshine and cool but not cold air. Some of the guests were walking outside on the myriad paths through the trees, before dinner was to be announced. The grooms were having their wedding photographs taken with the golden leaves and silver trunks of birch trees as a background. Gav hadn't stopped grinning all day, and Phil looked proud and glowing.

Jo didn't know Gav's other half very well, but he turned out to be quietly charming with a wicked sense of humour. After the ceremony, while welcoming all the guests into the reception, Gav had whispered to her a reminder that her invite was for two. Maureen had thrown her a knowing look at that. She had brought Frankie as her guest, and the two older women were having a marvellous party.

'Thanks,' Jo said, lifting the glass of

champagne in a mock toast. 'Where's Andy?'

'Gone to find the canapés. I did warn him that there's a huge wedding meal to come, but he said he wants to make the most of the day. How are you?'

'I wish everyone would stop asking me that,' Jo said, then shook her head. 'Sorry, I didn't mean that. Honestly, I'm fed up with my own moods. I shouldn't have come today.'

Stella looked shocked. 'You couldn't miss Gav's wedding. He'd be so upset if you weren't here.'

Jo sighed. 'You're right. Look, I'm out of sorts, but I mustn't let it get you down as well.'

'No chance of that,' Stella laughed. 'I'm so happy I could fly.'

'What did you think of Mum's announcement?'

'I was gobsmacked. But the money's going to come in very handy. It's not cheap going to college. But where are you going to live? I'll be okay in the student house; but you?'

'I'm going to buy my own flat.'

'What about Max?'

'I don't know. I'm not thinking about him today. I'm out to enjoy a good wedding and help Gav and Phil celebrate.'

'That's the spirit,' Stella said approvingly. 'I'll go and get some more champagne. Wait here.'

Jo watched her go, weaving in and out between the groups of Gav and Phil's friends and family. Men's heads turned as she went. Jo saw Andy catch her up and put his arm around her. Stella threw her bright head back and laughed. Jo caught the peal of it amongst the chatter. She felt inexplicably sad and yet peaceful, the emotions mingled and raw.

'Excuse me,' she mumbled, brushing past people and heading blindly for the grand entranceway. She put the champagne, untasted, down on a nearby table and continued to walk. The path took her in a winding fashion away from the house and down to a section of the woodland away from the main block. Here there was no one. Her shoes sank into a dense carpet of leaves, all russet and lemon, with shapes like starfish. A stream gurgled nearby and a single bird chirruped somewhere high above her.

She sat on a fallen log, not minding her dress. On a day like this, England was rather lovely. She ought to go back inside, she told herself, as they'd be starting the meal soon; but she had no appetite. She mulled over her phone call that morning. It was all settled: she had her mortgage in place, so now all she had to do was find a suitable flat. She should be excited.

She didn't need Maureen's money for a deposit, and she had no intention of going back to Germany. Max hadn't made contact with her, not an email or a letter or a phone call. The last time they'd spoken was when she phoned him after she returned home to let him know that Maureen was all right. It was up to him to make the next move.

The bird stopped singing abruptly. A stick cracked somewhere. Jo listened. The rush and play of the stream seemed louder. She looked up as a figure approached. The height and frame, so familiar . . . could it be . . . could it really be Max?

'Hello Jo.'

She stood up slowly, brushing leaves from her dress. Then, as if in a dream, she reached out to him, felt how real he was, and kissed him passionately.

She kept wanting to touch him to make sure he was real. Max must've felt the same way, because he held her hand and never let go.

'How did you find me?' she asked when at last their kisses stopped.

He traced her cheekbone with his finger and her nerves tingled. 'Your neighbour told me. I rang your doorbell so long that she got annoyed at the noise and came out to shout at me. Once I'd explained, she couldn't have been more helpful. She called me a taxi and gave me a map of where the manor house was.'

'No letters or phone calls. Why not?'

'You didn't call me either,' he chided gently. 'Maybe for the same reasons. It felt like it was over before it had begun.'

'What about Petra and Sylvie?' Jo asked.

He sat on the log beside her and she leaned right into him. His arm went around her automatically and he kissed her hair tenderly. 'Petra booked my flight here. Sylvie ordered her to do it.'

'I'm glad Sylvie came to her senses,' Jo said. 'Petra's more than able to understand that you need your life too.'

'And that I need you with me in that life,' Max said. 'I'm here to ask you to come back with me, Jo. Come back to Germany and let's see where this takes us.'

He hadn't said he loved her. What if she went back and it didn't work out between them? She'd have nothing. 'I'm about to buy a flat. I can't just up and away to Europe,' she said, 'any more than you can leave your vineyards and café.'

Max jumped up from the log. 'It's easier for you to leave. You can run your business anywhere. I can't.'

'But I can't leave Mum and Stella so far away,' Jo said. 'You're expecting too much from me.'

His grey eyes cooled and he stiffened. 'Then I've travelled here for nothing. I'm sorry I bothered you.' He walked away from her, out of the woods.

'Max! Where are you going?' Jo cried after him.

He turned back to her briefly. 'I'm staying in the town's hotel tonight. Then I'm going home tomorrow. There's nothing to keep me here now. Goodbye, Jo.'

She stood and watched him go. She wanted to run after him and cling to him and never let him go. But he wanted her to give up everything for him. And she was scared. She was in love with him, but he hadn't told her he was in love with her. What did Max really feel about her? She took a step after him and stopped. She wasn't going to beg for his love.

The guests were drifting back into the manor house. It was time for the meal. Jo walked back in too, her thoughts scattered. She found her place at one of the round tables with its crisp white linen tablecloth. She was seated next to Stella on one side and a man she didn't know on the other. As the courses were served, she ate numbly, unable to taste any of the food set before her.

When the meringue and strawberry dessert had been dished up and the plates emptied, Gav stood up to give his speech. Jo watched his gestures and Phil's laughter as the speech unfolded. She didn't hear a word of what he said, but she saw the love he had in every movement of his body, every expression on his face, as he spoke about Phil.

Beside her, Stella was whispering to Andy. He had his dark head next to hers and they were in a world of their own. Blindly, Jo groped for her silk shawl and bag. There were a few murmurs as she rose in the middle of Gav's speech. He halted for a brief second at the interruption. His gaze was full of warmth as he saw her leave. He gave an imperceptible nod and then carried smoothly on.

With Gav's approval, Jo's feet flew across the gravel and down to the road. She knew the hotel where Max was staying; it was only a few minutes' walk away. Her shoes pinched her feet as she ran, heedless of the stares, through the town.

There was a postbox on the street in front of the hotel. A man was standing at it, posting a letter. 'Max!' Jo shouted.

He lowered his hand, with the letter still in it. She reached him and tried to catch her breath. 'Max, don't go. We need to talk.'

He gave her the letter. 'When we were kids, we poured our hearts out to each other. Maybe I was better at writing my feelings than speaking them.'

Jo stared at it.

'Read it, please,' Max coaxed.

So, in the middle of the grey October street, with the traffic going past and a woman with a poodle wandering along on the opposite pavement, Jo read what Max had to say.

Dear Jo,

I didn't express myself very well in the woods. I was too overcome by seeing you again — your beautiful almond-coloured eyes and dark hair that I can't help but touch and kiss. And our kisses, they warm me even now.

But I did things badly. Instead of kissing you and holding your hand, instead of telling you with my body how I felt, I should have told you with my words.

I love you. I'm in love with you and always will be. It took me a while to realise it, but I think I've always loved you ever since we were kids writing our hearts to each other. Even before we met, I had found my soulmate in you.

I hope you feel the same way. I hope that when you get this letter, you'll come and find me and we can work out a way to be together. The castle and the vineyards and the café don't matter if I can't have you.

All my love,

Max.

'Were you really going to go home tomorrow?' Jo breathed after she had kissed Max again for good measure and told him she loved him too.

'No, I booked for a week. I reckoned you'd get my letter tomorrow and that one way or another I'd know my fate before the week was out.'

'That's crafty,' Jo murmured against the warm heat of his neck.

He cradled her to him. 'Not crafty, just the cunning of an experienced pen-pal. Timing is everything with letters.'

'Do you remember that our letters sometimes crossed in the post?' Jo said, laughing.

'Yes, we were so impatient to share more of what we felt that we didn't wait for each other's answers. But I always got a surge of happiness when your letters arrived.'

'Me too. Yours kept me going when I was growing up. There's only ever been one person for me, and that's you.'

'Shall we go into the hotel?' Max asked. 'It's getting cold, and we have more to discuss.'

'Would you mind if we went back to Gav and Phil's wedding? I rather ran out on them right in the middle of the speeches. The meal's over and the dancing will have started, but we can find a quiet corner to talk.'

'Can you walk in those heels?'

'I managed to run in them from the manor house,' Jo laughed, 'so hopefully they'll take me back too.'

'We know we love each other,' Max said, sounding almost bewildered at his good fortune, 'but can we agree on where we'll live? One of us is going to have to give up their home. As I said in my letter, I don't care where it is, as long as I've got you.'

'Oh Max, I was being silly. You can't give up your castle and the vineyards. They're your livelihood. But I can move my business out to Germany. It hadn't occurred to me that I'd have to move, that's all. It's a bit daunting moving to a new country where I don't speak the language, but I haven't been happy here since I left Germany. I keep imagining your castle and the lovely view and having drinks on the terrace. In fact, I'm homesick for it.'

'We can come back here for holidays, and it's not the other side of the globe.' He smiled.

'We'll work something out,' Jo agreed, tucking herself into his side as they walked back to the wedding.

'Now I have another question to ask you,' Max said.

She looked at him, wondering what else they needed to sort.

'Where will we get married?'

Epilogue

Jo lifted the tray of drinks and took it outside onto the terrace. The sunshine glinted off the glasses, and she slipped her sunglasses from her head to cover her eyes. In the café, Stella was singing off key as she brought out the cake, perfectly risen, from the oven.

'Is the café open today?' Maureen asked Max. She looked very summery in her rainbow-coloured dress and floppy straw hat. She lay back on the sun lounger and took the offered drink from Jo with a smile.

'I've closed it and the castle to visitors today,' Max said. 'After all, it's a special occasion when my mother-in-law makes her first visit to Germany.'

'And very nice it is too, although it's very hot.' Maureen fanned herself.

Jo pulled all the chairs in so that they could all sit together. Andy cut the cake into slices and put them onto plates.

'This is perfect,' Jo sighed as she slipped her hand into her husband's.

Max squeezed her fingers gently. 'It is wonderful to have your family here for the holidays.'

'Are Petra, Sylvie and Pierre joining us?'

'They'll be here soon, and you can practise some more of your excellent German,' Max said and kissed her.

'Flatterer,' Jo laughed and returned his kiss.

'Jo's joined the local choir and is singing in German,' Max told the others.

'You should teach me some,' Stella said. 'I've decided my café will have speciality German cakes. Frau Hiss is going to teach me some recipes while we're here.'

'And I might learn some words too,' Maureen said. 'Frankie and I are taking a cruise down the Rhine later this year and visiting some fairytale castles.'

At that moment Max's family arrived,

and introductions were made. Jo went back into the café to heat the kettle. Even though it was a hot day, Pierre liked strong black coffee. She took a moment to look around at the cosy scene that had played host to a variety of birthday parties and other celebrations in the ten months since she'd moved to Germany. Then her view shifted out through the open patio doors, beyond the terrace to the outline of the village with its red roofs and slender church spire and the dark shapes of the mountains beyond. It was a beautiful place to live, and she had no regrets.

Their wedding had taken place in her hometown church, at Maureen's insistence. Then Jo had packed her belongings and they'd returned to Eichstatt. It had been a smooth transition, and she'd managed to keep her business going online. Once her German was better, she hoped to gain some local customers too.

Besides, there was always work in the café, and in the vineyards, or showing tourists around the castle. She wasn't short of interesting things to do. Best of all, she was with Max every single day, and their love grew only more intense as they learned about each other's likes and dislikes. The only downside, Max had said, was there would be no more exchange of long-distance postcards and Christmas cards. Jo reckoned she could live with that.

Stella's laughter rippled in the air. She and Petra were sharing photographs. Jo wondered what the contents were. In a minute, when the coffee was ready, she'd go and join them and share their fun. Then she'd ask Sylvie how the boutique was faring and how Pierre's golf was going. And she'd make sure that Maureen was happy. She wanted her mum to return many times to share their life here.

And finally, she would go to her loving husband, Max, and wrap her arms around him.